Felix Chance

volume one

j.e. pittman

For Love

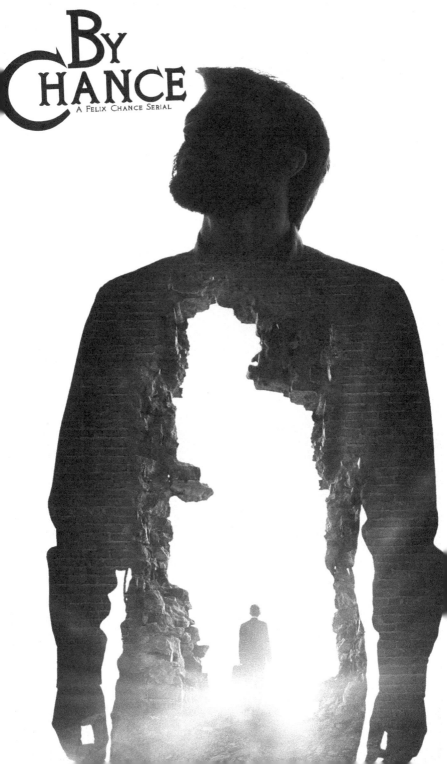

Mallorey's

PEOPLE WILL EAT ANYWHERE, it seems. So long as the food is tasty and, more importantly, they don't have to make it themselves.

Or so I found out when the sneezing man led me to Mallorey's. I looked up from the counter, briefly, to see the line of apparent customers snaking to the door before dashing back to the kitchen lest it all catch fire.

I don't actually work at Mallorey's, or any restaurant, and only sort of know what I'm doing. Well, I can make soup. A smidge of salad. Definitely not breadsticks, though.

"Grilled cheese and tomato," Molly called from the counter. That I can make.

"Ayo," I responded, sliding an aforementioned salad through the window and grabbing some bread for the slathering in a single motion. Most of the ingredients had been left prepped when I found the place, but I still had to hunt things down, like a cheese slice. "Cheese...cheese...are you cheese?" I sifted through the fridge stocked by someone else. "Aha! Cheese!" I said, peeling off a slice of something white.

The door opened and from outside came an overly loud 'achoo!' that likely could be heard on the moon.

Who needs a billboard when you've got the sneezing man? Best advertisement there is. Got me stuck behind the counter slinging soup and slathering bread to sizzle on the griddle.

It was a novel idea, Mallorey's. Let me rewind a bit.

You know how you just walk down the street, minding your own business, when suddenly your stomach rumbles and while you're thinking about soup, a guy sneezes and you look up just in time to catch a restaurant out the corner of your eye? And you go into said restaurant and it's entirely devoid of human life? But all the tables and chairs and plants are there just waiting for customers...and maybe some staff?

No? Just me?

Strange. Thought it might be a more common thing.

"How's the gazpacho coming, Felix?"

Molly. Sweet Molly. Mallorey's second customer and first employee, cause I guess I hired her? More like she had an idea to run with as people streamed in the door.

I pulled a can of red and a can of veg I'd left chilling in the freezer and dumped them in a bowl and sprinkled a little parsley on top. Presentation is everything.

She grabbed and dashed and I flipped the grilled and added the vitamin cheese.

Achoo.

More people came. And came.

And came.

How many people come to a restaurant that isn't even open? At no point did I put an open sign in the window, yet people kept showing up. We had no cash. No register. Molly had the bright idea to feature being cashless.

She had all the app thingies and one of those pixely codes. People loved it.

I just wanted some soup.

Now I'm saddled with a restaurant... by right of salvage? I guess?

Who leaves a restaurant stocked and unattended? I heard 'ghost kitchens' were a thing in covidtimes, but they didn't have tables or chairs. And who watered these plants? Were they ghosts, too?

A cop buddy of mine told me once he arrested some guys smoking pot out behind an IHOP. Turns out that IHOP was run by a grand total of three people at 1 o'clock in the morning. And all three of them were out back smoking.

Oops.

"Probably not pot," I crossed off my mental list.

"Hm?" Molly cocked her head.

"Just wondering why the door was unlocked." It was strange.

"Who cares," she grinned. Dimples showing in her cheeks. "We're up a grand so far."

"No shit? Guess people like soup."

"Glad I caught you now, aren't you?"

Red handed, in fact, from the tomato. She'd walked in as I took it upon myself to make a bowl of my own since no one was around to do it for me. She'd asked for lentil herself.

"I'm sorry, I don't think we have any," I'd said when she found me in the back. I'd tried to excuse myself, leaving the soup to fend for itself, but she blocked my path.

"You don't work here, do you?" Her blue eyes pierced me as her auburn hair flipped about while she confronted me. "Are you raiding the kitchen?" Her tone highly accusatory.

"Are you Mallorey? I'm sorry. I'm famished and you weren't here and the door was unlocked and everything was ready..." I trailed off my string of lame excuses as she began to laugh.

"Not Mallorey." She left the proclamation hanging there as she appraised me, the kitchen, the whole situation, arms crossed as she thought. "Molly," she said, suddenly following up. "And I'm hungry too, duh. Where is everyone?"

"Aliens?" I gestured memely.

She giggled. It sounded like sweet, tinkly bells, I thought. But it was the door.

Achoo!

"Be right back," she brightened with what I now knew was an idea forming. "Hi!" she beamed. "Welcome to Mallorey's..." and she began conning the new arrivals into sending her digital money.

Apparently this was a grand idea. And counting.

"What kind of cheese was that?" Molly popped her head around the corner. "Twelve wants to know."

"Who's twelve?" I drew a blank at her question.

"Table twelve," she said, growing a bit impatient. "Grilled cheese and tomato. Said it was the best grilled cheese ever and wanted to know."

"The tables have numbers?" I was still a few steps behind the conversation. I knew most eateries numbered them but hadn't thought these had such. Besides, Molly was by herself out there. *Maybe I should hire another customer?*

"I numbered them," she said as I mused the idea and dismissed it. The situation *was* slightly abnormal and questions...

"Hey, excuse me, I've got a pickup for Tollison," the Doordash guy interrupted. "Hello?"

"Are we..?"

"Did you..?" We stepped on each other as our eyes snapped to.

My mouth worked a gape for an answer that didn't come. Molly to the rescue yet again.

"Oh sure," she charmed back out into the dining room. "I'm sorry, our app is glitching. Which one was that?" I leaned close to the corner to hear.

The rude dude I now intensely disliked sighed and annoyedly flicked his phone for a second to look.

"Says here: Vegan patty melt with a side of onion rings, extra mustard. Diet soda." He listed off all the things I didn't have.

"Oh dear," Molly sweetened her voice a half-octave higher. "That's just all wrong," she grabbed his phone to examine it closer, leading the dasher to the door. "They must not have updated our menu," she faded away.

Achoo. Open and shut.

"Well then," she returned, chipper and bright, having dealt handily with that problem. "Cheese?" She quirked her eyebrow, returning to the previously scheduled topic.

"Cheese," I shrugged. "Cheese is cheese."

"For the sake of our friendship," she clutched her wounded heart, "I'll pretend you did not just say that." She swept her hand melodramatically to her forehead as she winked and left.

We're friends? I had no idea. Note to self: Don't bring up lacking cheese knowledge in front of Molly.

Orders came and went as the day wore on. The soup cans ran low. People were still — Achoo — coming in.

"Should I run to the store?" Maybe there's an app. "Hey Molls," I called her 'Molls' to see how the nickname tasted.

"Don't call me that." She snapped. "What?"

"Sorry," I flinched. "We're out of soup cans. Among your many apps is there one to summon more?"

The back door clicked open just as I finished asking. Our heads snapped to see a pair walk in most unassumingly and then stop cold.

Frozen for a moment, we all stood there looking at one another. Obviously they hadn't expected anyone to be squatting in the restaurant and, likewise taken unawares, we were busted. Shit.

They moved first. The guy took out a knife. Oh shit. Oh shit.

"We're here for the sink," she said as he silently began cutting the caulk from the backsplash. For this — not separating me from any of my other parts — I was grateful.

"Okay," I said matter of factly as I motioned Molly back to the dining room door. "Sure, go ahead. I was done with it anyway," I trailed off, backing away even though there were still dishes in said sink. Knife dude turned the water off last I looked.

Molly and I passed through the bustling dining room full of soup eaters and salad munchers and gooey grilled cheese savorers not making eye contact and not stopping for the questions that followed us to the door.

Achoo!

We both jumped as the man who began all of this snapped our too-wound springs. Molly yelped.

"Bless you." I told the man on reflex as I checked behind us to see if the sink repo team was coming for us next.

"Thank you," the sneezing man said. "Been sneezing all day and not a word from anyone," he shook his head and walked off, his curse apparently broken with my blessing.

Molly and I shared a look and kept getting.

After a bit we broke the silence. "What the hell was that?" We lost it, laughing until we collapsed on a bench. This attracted many stares but we just couldn't care.

Exhaustion set in and I just stared at the passing clouds in silence. The sun would soon set on this weirdass day.

"Most delicious grilled cheese sandwich ever," she read. "Bursting with sweet flavor and extra gooey goodness. Paired with a pedestrian tomato soup. 4 stars."

"Yelp?" Always with the apps. I shut my eyes.

"Yep," Molly nodded, though I could not see. "Muenster," she guessed.

"Cheese." I risked her feigned wrath.

"I guess we can't do it again tomorrow." She said instead, a little halfhearted.

"I don't think Mallorey's has a tomorrow."

"Sadness." And it showed.

It was a shame, really. I've done lots of odd jobs here and there. Pickup work. Gardener. Handyman. Mechanic. Even a house painter, though that did not go exactly as expected, but restaurateur was a first. That had been fun and I got a new friend out of the deal.

I looked over at Molly and saw her for the first time. Really saw her. Saw her without the distractions and constant flood of adrenaline rushing through everything. She really was sad that Mallorey's had no tomorrow.

Her stomach rumbled as embarrassment switched places with sadness.

"Did you ever eat?"

"No," she admitted, "I forgot to, you know, like in the rush of it all."

"Well let's go." I popped up from the bench, hunger renewed.

"Go where?"

I swept a right bow and offered her my hand. "Why, anywhere we don't have to make the food ourselves."

The Huxley

THERE ARE WORDS IN my brain that only other words will unlock. These, however, had no such keys contained within their bloated pages. I sat the book down with great disappointment and shall not name such here as a courtesy to fellow authors or ghost-authors writing under a brand name or mayhap an AI?

Those are a thing now, apparently. Feed in the works of ten-thousand cigar chomping monkeys churning away at ten-thousand-and-one typewriters — I hear Monty can type with his feet, too. Scholar, that one — and the programs will shit some feces out on the screen.

Would explain the torrents of drek deluging e-ink displays everywhere in the ceaseless scroll. Not that every piece has to be a grand work of literature, but it should at least know how to put a participle past present and that picking cousin gerund for the job can be tricksy.

"Whatcha doin?" I squatted down next to the low table Molly worked from cross legged in the floor by the fire. Having found nothing of literary interest, I'd decided to bug her.

"Puzzling," she replied, a piece held to her lips in thought.

"I know you're puzzling, but what occupies your time?" Molly was many things, a mystery among them. The look she shot needed no deciphering.

"Placing tiny pieces of cardboard cut in circuitously interlocking fashion by perhaps a press, or now-a-days a laser-sans-shark, into their original arrangement so as to form this picture of a kitten," Molly wandered verbaciously as she waved her hand over a box lid depicting said kitten. Her head cocked back and forth with the rhythm of the words she clipped out staccato.

"But you already have this picture of the kitten." I smarmed and smirked, holding up the puzzle-box lid.

"Silence," she snipped, albeit playfully, as I sat across from her by the cozy fire crackling away in the overly-large hearth.

Overly-large by comparison at any rate. We were but two travelers in the night come to The Huxley and the hearth within could easily host a dozen or more, running the width of my height.

For us, instead of large logs alight to crackling embers, it contained but a merry mound of sticks stuck in at odd angles. Neither of us were particularly good at making a fire. Burning things, sure, that was easy. But a properly laid fire was a work of art and testament to skillful wood-and-or-home-craft.

Our little bonfire, on the other hand, was an abstract piece. Impressionist at best.

"Should we be using up their firewood," Molly had asked when I assembled the masterwork.

"You danced about in the rain. They said make ourselves at home," I'd said, putting two and two together to make fire.

We'd stopped at The Huxley when hunger set in while a detour around a rockslide had us the wrong side of lost in mountains which had not taken the latest update to the GPS. It was here or a BBQ joint straight out of *Fried Green Tomatoes* and I didn't much feel like being an accessory after the fact — The Huxley it was.

The valet had seemed as surprised when we pulled up as we were there *was* a valet. I finally handed over the keys when Martin — he'd so named himself — had assured us he was, in fact, the valet, and he would park it within view of the door.

And to his credit, he did.

I'd stood at the door and watched the entire thirty seconds it took him to pull the T-bird down the driveway, a little to the left into a small graveled lot, and walk back. He'd waved as he got out.

"Your key, sir," Martin had bowed slightly as he proffered the key. I suppose since I'd stood there waiting distrustfully, he thought it best not to keep my key at the valet stand. Instead he kept his hand out, coughing ever so slightly until I realized he wanted a tip. I sighed and slipped him a dollar. No favors.

"I thought you were the con artist here," I muttered to Molly and went inside before Martin could protest the small gratuity.

"Should have tipped him more," Molly snapped me out of memory as if reading my wandering thoughts. She placed a piece of the kitten in place, the left ear, and took up another. Her slightly accusatory tone hinted that she'd not now be exorbitantly damp had the valet remained to fetch the car.

"You'd still have danced among the drops," I countered. She'd laughed like a maniac, drenching herself more and more in the after dinner downpour, all while coaxing me to make a run for the Thunderbird. I'd had to pull her inside when lightning kachowed too near.

"Likely." Her eyes twinkled with the mischief I knew she held barely in check, yearning to be free. She placed another piece of the kitten. A paw. "I mean, why not, no one was watching."

"Kinda the point," I circled back. "Where is everyone?"

Molly considered another piece of the puzzle. "The lake." She said it with such certitude, such definitive confidence that I almost didn't question.

"We passed that lake coming up here and it was empty," I said.

"That's *a* lake, not *the* lake." Another certitude.

"There's a difference?"

"Yes. It's in the manual," she said. Molly began reading from an invisible book. "Page three-hundred-and-seventy-four," she made up, "'On the occasion of long holiday weekends,' such as we find ourself on now," she looked down her nonexistent glasses at me in an aside, "'the civilized individuals shall go to *the lake* nearest as indicated by the map on page eighty-nine.' And that page shows all the qualifying lakes within regional driving distance."

"What's a *qualifying* lake then?" I played along.

"Oh, it has to be fairly large. One on which you can hardly see the opposite shore. Several docks for pontoons. Approximately ninety minutes away. Only back roads to get there. Surrounded by super sketch gas stations, nothing nice. No national chains by county ordinance — ruins the ambiance."

"No clean bathrooms then?"

"God no," she laughed. "You *have* to hold it."

"Is that in the manual, too?" Molly's laugh sparkled. Her wit was something to behold and I was happy to have the distraction from this isolation. *Where* had *everyone gone?*

We didn't wait for a table, certainly, but the restaurant hadn't been empty either. There were, in fact, several patrons enjoying much heartier fare than soup-al-a-can or a mystery grilled cheese and I was glad to soon be among their ranks.

But slowly they'd vanished. By ones and twos as the food was finished.

Wanda and Todd — the couple across the room whose names we didn't know and so called them Wanda and Todd — left after a brief spat that ended with Wanda slapping her napkin on the table and storming off. Flustered, Todd threw down some bills and quickly went after.

Sir Ian Phlegmy there writing at the bar — who had a thick cough his whisky couldn't quell —gave up with an exasperated sigh once his characters stopped speaking. Terrible when that happens. Tragic. He'd drawn many looks askance as he hacked — as if to say 'stay home' or 'wear a mask' — from the Amys seated nearby.

Amy S. and Amy B. and Amy O. — all of a generation that didn't have the greatest naming variety — each fussed over the bill after fretting the 'rona, trying to treat the others on their apparent girls' weekend while Aimee — cleverer spelling than the rest — had paid the check when she'd excused herself to the restroom around the corner.

Mason — who could have been Martin's twin, but wasn't — appeared with our own check and a fresh bottle of red. "No rush, enjoy your evening," he'd said as he left the bill and bottle.

Molly snapped the code before I could even reach the slip and squared up in yet another app. "What?" She looked over her phone at my thwarted chivalry. "Don't worry, I used our soup money." She clattered the phone down and took up her glass for a toast. "To soup!"

"And cheeses, grilled and not," I clanked.

"To cheese!" She shouted the cheers.

"Shh-sh-sh-heh." I tried to admonish her through my laughter, but failed. Not that it mattered, the tables had trickled away with none to replace them. Only the bartender remained behind, polishing glasses with a hiss from the latte steamer.

"Maybe it's a trap," Molly said, dropping another piece of the puzzle in place.

Eventually even the bartender had vanished behind the bar, never to return. No Mason or Martin inside or out. No one at the front desk because apparently there were no guests — everyone having read this manual which dictated gathering at *the* lake.

"A trap for who, or what?" For having mentioned it, Molly seemed decidedly unconcerned that it might be some sort of trap. Although nothing about The Huxley screamed *trap*, tourist or otherwise.

"Well. Probably not for us." The pieces of kitty fell into place more rapidly now that the placement options dwindled. "Why don't you belong here? I don't think we were expected."

"We didn't even expect ourselves," I agreed.

"No favors or gifts. Good on you for tipping, lousy as it was..." she continued working through the puzzle. "You go here. You go there."

"I could have parked it mysel..." She cut me off with a forestalling hand as she finished the kitten.

"Charming little trap, this," she said, popping to her feet. "Now let's be off before the fae change their mind and Van Winkle us." Molly headed for the unlocked front door, turning the knob to the left.

"Yes. Quite charming," I said, looking at the drawing room where we'd waited out the rain. The storm had faded and the fire died down to but motes and embers. I followed Molly, lingering to look around once more as we departed The Huxley. It had been a pleasant evening. "We'll have to come back some time."

"No way we'll ever find this place again." Sure of her words, Molly spun on her heel to walk backwards down the darkened lane. There was no question. No doubt. "Let's just hope a hundred years haven't passed our night away. Eh?"

The Byron Building

STARTING OFF WITH A coffee and a clipboard she swiped from the ledge along Drip Feed, a minorly pretentious coffee joint, Molly had set our course in the name of a few jollies to be obtained from the Byron Building.

Let me lay the scene.

You see, Molly likes old buildings, apparently. *Really* likes them. As in, well, you know. Also apparently, it's some sort of condition and as such she identifies as Archisexual. It's a thing. Google it if you dare. I currently can't.

Anyway. Who am I to judge what floats her boat? But I didn't know this at the time she lifted the inspector's clipboard. In fact, I didn't even know it was the inspector's clipboard or what was to be inspected until...

"Sam, I presume?" A perky blond in a red business casual get up approached us from nowhere, her eyebrows quizzical. "Gwen said you'd be over today to do a sign off." She leaned in and smiled a fake smile as she pointed out the sharpied letters S A M on the coffee Molly held. Like I said, perky.

"Guilty," Molly confirmed, checking her drink. Her 'Sam' laugh was equally fake.

Of something, I thought. I still don't know if Molly knew who's mocha latte she'd lifted and just ran with it or? I'm beginning to think she knew *exactly* who's.

Which leads me now to being locked in the dark of a *Duck-and-Cover* era fallout shelter sixty-five feet below the Byron Building. Plenty of time to reflect.

The mirrored walls lining the halls of the historic Byron Building had speckled a bit with age as old silvered mirrors tend to do. I checked my teeth for breakfast quiche as Sunbeam — I never caught her actual name — swayed along to her office to then introduce us to Gus — whose name was handily on a tag — who was to be our sagacious guide on today's journey.

"The Byron is undergoing historic preservation and revitalization as part of the city's Centerpiece Plan," she'd said by way of introduction to the task. "As such, we've worked diligently to maintain the original charm while modernizing..." I trailed off listening, instead preferring to look.

Sunbeam left us. I was sad. Molly was giddy. Gus was Gus.

"A'right, where you want to start," Gus asked. I'm pretty sure he came with the building, might be the same vintage.

"Lights and Exits?" Molly referenced the nicked clipboard. I got the feeling she'd done this before.

"Come on." I got the feeling Gus had shown lots of idiots around before.

As we walked, I wondered if his shuffled feet had been in part responsible for these marble thresholds. Swooped is the word that pops in my head, I have no idea if that's the real word for where the straight stone dips in the middle. But that's the word that comes to mind. Stone stairs do it too, from countless passings.

"Gimme a hand," Molly said. She was reaching for a tiny black button on the bottom of an exit light up high. Gus had gone somewhere.

"What exactly are you doing?" Molly jumped for the button.

"Testing emergency exit lights," she said confidently. "But I don't have a stick, lift me!"

"I can see that," I said, walking over. "Rephrasing: *why* are you testing emergency exit lights?"

"Because they need testing," she waved her clipboard at me. "Look, just back me here," she said.

Why the hell not? Molly's voice had held an edge I hadn't heard before.

"Thanks, it's been far too long," she said as I bent to give her a lift. Then we plunged into darkness — reminiscent of my current predicament.

Molly had made it about halfway up to my shoulders, clutching precariously to my protesting throat as her purloined clipboard smacked my face. The floods — which I had been looking directly at — flashed on to wash away the darkness.

Blinded by the light, I fell, taking Molly with me.

What Gus thought when he came back upon us, he declined to share. His only reaction was an "Uh huh," as his flashlight swept over us lying on the floor.

"Emergency lights, check." Molly ticked a box on Sam's clipboard and we carried on floor number three.

The third floor was a jumble of boxes. Veritable jumble, I say. Boxes of the office sort joined by curves, with smaller boxes tucked in at all angles along the marooned walls. Perfect for playing hide and seek, perfect for privacy, not perfect for scooting about. Molly made a face.

"What a death trap!" Molly exclaimed. "This won't do at all!"
She waved Sam's clipboard for emphasis. The hall off the left
of the elevator was filled with junk and boxes and still more
junk beside the other junk and I'm sure there was probably
more junk underneath. I think Molly actually twitched at the
sudden stuff.

Gus grunted and began moving clutter from the halls. "Told
them not'a put that shit there." He grumbled again. These
were most words I'd heard from him yet, all strung together
as he slid the offending detritus out of the way. "Not s'pose
to."

"No, they're not," she agreed and went off on a new tangent.
"Why would you do this to such a beautiful space?" She
actually huffed. The list of transgressions grew as she
threaded her way across the stone floors. "Drop tile!? I bet
these ceilings are gorgeous. You can't even see the friezes
with these build outs." She gaped about with incredulity.

Gus nodded and gave a short grunt. I hadn't been around
him enough to decipher these micro-expressions but Molly
seemed to speak his language.

"I know, not your fault," she consoled. "What'd the monsters
hide?"

"Tin." Gus pointed straight up. "Mermaids." He pointed off
to the side, where I presumed the — friezes? whatever they
are — would be located. Molly has the thing for buildings,
not me.

Molly hissed through her teeth, making notes on the
clipboard. She scratched slightly harder than necessary.

Ding, we returned to the elevator bay.

"Original charm my ass," Molly muttered as the doors shut.
Gus grunted.

The fourth floor presented a new challenge, being still under
construction and quite dusty. Plastic flapped in the hall

covering the torn out openings in walls that actually seemed to originally belong.

I knew we were in for a treat when I spotted an upturned bucket with a brick on top holding down a note which read: 'Whatever you do, don't move this brick. It will get loose.'

"Is that to code?" I pointed it out to Molly, who examined it seriously.

"No, just good sense." She nodded and bobbed along, less offended by this floor despite the indecent state we found it in. In fact, she seemed rather captivated by the naked structure beneath the skimpy, sheer plastic.

Molly lifted the sheet gingerly, teasing her way to the exposed conduit beneath. "Why don't you go taste for lead," she said, stroking the delicate bends in the metal.

"You mean test?" I said.

"If there's lead, the chips will be slightly sweet," she said distractedly. I guess she did mean taste. "Put a bittering agent in in the 70s to keep kids from eating the chips." She was lost, amorously admiring the craftsmanship. I left her to her predilections.

I really shouldn't be left unsupervised. I seem to get in over my head that way. Looking at my current predicament I couldn't help but think I should make better decisions. Like not meeting up with perky blondes who fake more than the blonde. Deirdre had tried to warn me, I think.

She's the fortune teller I met after I wandered off on my own.

"Welcome, lost wanderer. Welcome to Madame Zestra, Seer of your true heart. Few things escape my gaze." Her green eyes pierced me where I stood, pinned like a bug to a shadowbox board. "Come, come," she beckoned me closer, waving her hands over her crystal ball.

Her eyes never left mine as I stepped closer through the construction plastic. At the time I didn't think it off that a palm reader would set up shop on a floor under construction. The foot traffic was horrible.

"Choose your question wisely, you get but one," she continued. "Should you pay the price," she graciously waved my attention to the side, breaking the emerald gaze but briefly, directing me to a ubiquitous QR code. Everyone had them these days, even two-bit psychics. "I take Venmo, CashApp, Crypto. However you like to pay, I take." She delivered her spiel with a well practiced tongue.

"'What the hell, why not?'" She spoke in parody of my thought. That one was a gimme. "Tell you what," she said, sensing hesitance. "You feel in need, the universe compels me, and it is never wrong." Her curly black hair held back with a floral band shook with certainty. "Come, come," she beckoned me closer in whisper.

She was good. Fantastic presence despite the odd set up. She would do well once the reno was done and people started filtering through. I humored her and sat.

Her switch flipped.

The face of 'Madame Zestra' shook and made that sound heeby-jeeby-afflicted cartoons make. I can't quite put the letters together for the proper onomatopoeia. Her hands and arms and spine seemed to all shake free.

"Like wow, oh my gosh. Hi!" She perked up, a complete one-eighty from her presence before. Gone were the shining emeralds replaced by a more willowy hazel. Her smile bright. Her presence warm and gentle like a summer breeze.

"Hmm hm mmm hmmm." She hummed the snatch of triggered song while she covered the crystal ball with a silken cloth.

As I said, I sat. She shuffled.

I sat some more.

The cloth had previously been covering the tarot deck she now shuffled, seemingly oblivious to my presence.

I cleared my throat. "Madame Zestra?"

Nothing.

"Madame Zestra?" I tried again as she hummed along to her shuffling. She ignored me still.

No, that's not quite right. Ignoring implies malice. Willful neglect of one's presence. There was no malice in her actions.

Obviously the cards were busy speaking to her and maybe I should leave a message? Unsure how to proceed, I made a move to leave.

A card flew to the table. There was a picture of four sticks on it. She pulled it to the side upside down.

"Conflicts. Instability. Shaky." She tsked as she said it. "No roots." Her eyes flickered over me, darting around at perhaps only things she saw? Nice affectation to her act. She took a breath as a cloud passed her sunshine smile.

Another card flipped out of her hands. This one featuring a big bolt of lightning zapping a stone tower. I looked closer and there were tiny figures falling off the sides. Creepy. Probably not good.

"Oh my." Her tone confirmed my suspicion. "Chaos. Money Lost. Upheaval."

"Yippee," I drolled. Her eyes snapped to mine.

"All is not yet lost," she bubbled. Some laugh in the face of danger. Apparently she giggled at chaos.

A final card flipped from the deck. This she toyed with for a moment, flipping it one way then the other before she placed it with the rest, upside down like the first. Depicted on this one was a shapely woman crowned with gold. She held a star in her hand. Like the kind you'd draw as a child? Five points made of lines.

"Self-absorbed gold digger." If a flower could spit, that was the face it made.

"Not a fan?"

"You have terrible taste," she admonished with cheer. Even her negative comments reeked with positivity. "Tea?"

"Is it blueberry hibiscus?" I pulled a random tea from the memory banks.

"Fresh out, sadly," she laughed. "I'm having Rooibos."

"Make it two." I was up for trying it. I like tea, but like cheese, tea is tea. Whatever's put in front of me is usually good.

I held my silence gingerly as 'Madame Zestra' moved about the cozy space. Code word for small, but lovingly adorned, cozy is. She pulled out two paper hot cups imprinted with a steaming cup of joe on the side and two small tea bags with a reddish brown tea inside and one electric kettle that had been steaming to the side. These she combined in equal parts, one for her and one for me, before returning the kettle to its base which sat next to an oddly bulbous plastic bag.

It appeared to me that the bulbous bag was in fact of the grocery sort repurposed atop part of a deconstructed AC to form an ad hoc mini-fridge. From within her contrivance she withdrew a school lunch size carton of milk which she brought to the table along with honey.

"Clever," I said, pointing to the bag resuming its bulbous shape as it refilled with cold air.

"I make do." She took the warm cup in her hands and inhaled the fragrance of steeping tea. "Five minutes," she said. I supposed that's how long it needed.

"Since we have time, Madame Zestra..." I trailed off hoping she would fill in the gaps of her soothsaying act.

"Deirdre," she said, her hand to her chest. "Madame Zestra is my guide," she motioned to the air around her. "She can be a bit theatrical." Deirdre's bubbly laugh lit in her hazel eyes.

"I really hadn't noticed," I smirked. "Okay, Deirdre then..." I motioned to the cards still laying on the table, my eyebrow questioning.

"You have *terrible* taste," Deirdre said again, her eyes lingering on the Queen card. "But I think you know that and you do it anyway." She looked up at me with a hint of sadness. "Self destructive," she said, pointing to the second card to fall with a sharp purple nail. Perfectly manicured.

"Bingo," I said. I did. I won't deny it. "So do I meet this gold digger soon or do I know her already?" I leaned in closer seeing if I recognized anyone from the face card. Maybe it would speak to me too?

"Oh wooooow." Her eyes rolled as she laughed, sitting back in her chair to smell the tea again. The Rooibos was rather fragrant. "Deflecting. Nice."

I shrugged. It'd worked so far in my life, might as well continue. "Do you get strays wandering by a lot up here?" I looked around at all the construction she was nestled between. Ad hoc mini-fridge. Plastic sheeting for a door and, it would seem, at least one wall. The rest were covered with blankets and quilts and star patterned sheets printed with some astrological names and signs. Christmas lights accented the ceiling and flowers adorned the corners.

"I like the energy," Deirdre said. "Most of my sessions are conducted online." She pointed to the goose arm curving over the table. I'd thought it was a reading lamp at first, since it was making a cone of light, but, in fact, it held a phone. "Like and subscribe if you feel so moved," she radiated positively.

"Many subscribers then?"

"Those who need the message find it when needed." She sipped her tea to test before adding a dab of honey and a dollop of milk. I guess it was ready.

"Now who's deflecting?"

She continued sipping her tea and radiating positivity at me. How can people do that? It was remarkable. You can just sit there and look at them and they just seem happy and content and fulfilled and blah. I needed to learn that trick.

"You don't need tricks. Just manifest what you need. Open yourself and be receptive." She spread her hands wide, turning her palms up in a practiced motion as she breathed in deeply.

That one wasn't a gimme. *Get out of my head!* I thought loudly, just in case.

She tilted her head to the side and smiled a bit.

"You've come untethered," she said. "That's the core message I'm receiving for you." She gathered the cards back to the deck with a sweep of her nimble fingers. Each nail sported a different color.

"I've always been fine without attachments," I said. I'd drifted around a while, true, but I liked it that way.

"This is different," she said. "Unraveling." She waved her fingers in a vague motion, like plucking at threads.

I have terrible taste. Deirdre was right about that. Shoulda listened. I wonder what else she was trying to tell me over tea. Rooibos is tasty by the way, in case you were wondering. Wish I had some now.

"Can't you do something about this?" Sunbeam shrilled her repeated complaint.

Cringe. Terrible taste indeed.

The Bunker
@Byron

YEP. WE WERE TRAPPED in the fallout shelter below the Byron. The door stuck shut when it slammed home and there was no alternative means of egress.

Gonna say this one doesn't tick the box.

"Can't we do something about this?" She cornered me on the fourth floor after my tea with Deirdre. "Do you really have to write us up?" Her tone was playful, wanting something.

Ah. Gus spilled the beans about floor three. He'd been quieter than usual. No grunts of approval, or were they disapproval? I couldn't tell. Sunbeam, however: I'd seen her play before.

Molly was off who knows where ogling who knows what — conduit, ductwork, window leading — so Sunbeam moved on her next likely target. Me.

"Well," I hedged. "Maybe not."

"Oh, I'd be so appreciative!" Her pearly whites glistened as she flashed a smile, stepping closer. Veneers, too. I bet Sunbeam wasn't even her real name. "I'd hate to bring everything to a halt over some silly boxes," she patted my chest and laughed, tossing her hair back with a flip. Classic.

I raised my eyebrows and gave in to the fake flirt. "Care to discuss it somewhere more private?" I smiled. "Say, your office?"

Gus grunted. That one probably disapproval.

"I have a better idea," she perked, brushing against my elbow. Warm. "Follow me."

Sunbeam threaded her arm through mine and pulled close as she began to walk me away. Her hips swayed close to mine.

She knew her stuff. Every move she made calculated to get what she wanted. I was just along for the ride. Leaning her body across mine, she pressed down.

"We have this fantastic new project idea I want your take on." We went down. Ding. "I call it The Bunker@Byron," she said, leading me across the lobby to a door marked with a radiation warning.

"Do I need my Geiger counter?" She tittered at my lame joke as she opened the shelter door. Why is that so effective? I mean, I knew what she was doing, but it still worked like a charm.

I followed her down the darkened steps. Like I said: along for the ride.

"Don't worry, I have protection," she purred, turning up the heat. The door clicked shut.

I felt like we were under the bucket with a brick on top.

"What bucket?" Sunbeam was significantly cloudy by this point. Her face verged on thunderhead that could break any second.

"With the sign that said 'don't let it out.'" Had I been talking out loud?

"Nevermind." She banged the door. That seemed to be her go-to solution. "Don't you have some sort of tool you can use to get us out?" Frustration.

"Already used the only tool I've got on me." If you could verbally waggle your eyebrows, I did.

Bang bang bang"...not very well..." Under her breath. But not far enough. Our tittering days were done, it would seem.

"Most just offer a bribe," I countered.

She gave me the look. The one that makes your hindbrain club the rest senseless and revs the engine. Close enough to count, her two-hundred-and-thirty-seven eyelashes fluttered at me. Sunbeam then turned the allure in her voice back on as she whispered close. "Why spend the money when I have other assets at my disposal." Click. Her teeth snapped by my ear. Her assets brushed against my chest.

Point proven she stepped away and resumed banging the door. "Hello!? Gus? Anyone?"

"If it's bomb proof, it's probably sound proof, too."

"You have any better ideas?" I didn't.

Bang bang BANG.

CRASH.

This from the other side of the bunker, source lost in shadow.

"That's where I come in," Molly called from the darkness. "Keeper of the bright ideas, I am." She flicked on her phone light.

"Where *did* you come in?" More importantly, we could get out!

"Next door," she hooked a thumb over her shoulder. Behind her, Gus grunted. His light appeared in the opening. "Well, not door, exactly." She looked down at the rusted iron plate she stood on that had presumably made the CRASH sound. "The boiler room." Molly waved us in.

Sunbeam and I followed through the opened hole in the wall, stepping into a narrow passage barely big enough to squeeze through. She had to suck in her chest.

"How did you find this?" I emerged into said room in which a defunct boiler was indeed located. While it loomed in steely silence, its successor hummed and pinged and let us know we were unwelcome. Like a cat, it hissed as we encroached on its territory. The pipes around us clanged against their mounts.

"I was inspecting the electric when I came on these darlings leading through the floor so I shimmied down to see where they went," she stroked the pipes lovingly. "And found this grand old man." She patted her new friend.

Ancient — something a grandfather might have built — silenced pipes spread everywhere, some vanishing up into the Byron leading the way for their new fit brethren, and more dove down below to where elder things held sway.

"How long were you in there?" I pulled Molly to the side.

"Long enough." She actually winked at me. "I'm still writing her up."

"You're not even an inspector!" I whispered with imperative, trying not to give up the jig. Sunbeam was mad enough as is. Who knew what she'd do if she knew.

"Details," Molly said dismissively. "Look, we both got our respective rocks off, I'd call that a win. Let's just let the endorphins do their thing." Molly smiled at me.

"Both?" She did have that heady, post-coital look. Her hair mussed. "I'm not even going to ask."

"Good, because we have bigger problems." Molly sobered seriously. So much for the endorphins. "It's loose." Dun-dun-dun!

Or so she thought I'd react. Instead. "What's loose?" I had no idea.

"Something's loose?" Sunbeam chose that moment to pay attention. She'd been in collusion with Gus about making a pass through to the bunker so she could get her speakeasy. "What's loose? Your screw?"

Ah hahaha, so funny. I really wanted to say that. But I let it slide.

"So you know that bucket..."Molly began, "that said 'don't let it out' or something to that effect," she waved dismissively.

"You let it out?" Gus with the words now. His give-no-fucks attitude left by the wayside.

"It was scritching at the bucket and mewling with its little voice. It sounded cute and I wanted to pet it..."

"You let it out..." Gus again, this time without the inflection.

"What? Why is 'out' bad?" Sunbeam clouded in confusion. "Was it bugs? Bed bugs? Please don't tell me it's bed bugs." She turned between Molly and Gus, earnestly hoping it wasn't bugs. I guess she didn't like bugs. "If you let bedbugs loose in my building, so help me..."

"So I lifted the brick and asked it nicely — whatever it was because I didn't know at the time — asked it not to run off and to let me pet it." Molly actually toed the ground like some school child called to task. She looked so young.

"You asked it nicely. And you didn't even know what you were letting out? What if it had been bugs?" Gus had waved her off the bug thing, sending some sort of short hand they only spoke to let her know it wasn't bugs. At least, I didn't hear any verbal communication about the not-a-bug-ness of the situation.

Molly rounded on Sunbeam, hand on hip. "He was scared and trapped under a bucket!" Irate. "And he *was not* happy about the whole situation, to say the least."

"Besides," she continued. "I was done and you were faking your second orgasm by that time, so I just crawled back out the way I came, so really it's all your fault, the both of you."

Molly did a damn good job of turning it back on us. Deflectors up. Absolving herself of sin. Deftly laying blame like a mason lays bricks. Sunbeam's mouth worked in vain, something she likely was unused to.

I was impressed.

"Okay okay." Time to head this conflict off. "What exactly got loose?"

"Well, I don't know exactly, but it looked like a fox." Molly held her hands up about yay wide. "A teeninsy one."

Gus grunted, not in agreement, and looked around. Uneasy.

"I didn't get a good look — or to pet it — since it just bolted once the bucket was removed." She seemed arguably more disappointed about the lack of petting. I learned more and more about Molly every day. Mysterious as she was, I was slowly fitting pieces together. "But it definitely wasn't a rodent and had red hair."

"Great. Swell. A ginger." I had a thing for gingers. It never ended well.

"Soulless," Gus said, in maybe agreement.

"Well it sounds to me like you two need to find this vermin you released into my building and remove it from the premises since you've admitted responsibility." It was Sunbeam's turn for hand on hip indignance. Fickle bitch.

Tempted to just give up the ghost and get out of there, I opened my mouth to speak. The sex hadn't been that good for me either. Not enough to put up with this attitude. Molly had other ideas.

As I crawled through the space between floors, I began to question the brightness of the ideas she was keeper of.

"You know, you'd probably fit through here easier than I do," I called back. "Remember your shimmy days of not too many hours ago? Nooks and crannies are your forte." My limbs kept getting tangled as I tried to move.

"That's entirely *not* the point here," Molly said from the safety of her post by the exit shaft. "I *could* easily climb in there but then I wouldn't be here to catch the little darling as it runs from the big scary man." She held a laundry bag open. One slightly larger than the bucket we'd originally seen upon the fourth floor. "That's you, by the way. Be scary. Grar." I heard her pantomiming from the cramped nook I rested in.

No sign of a teeinsy red fox. Part of me was glad as I didn't relish the idea of having my eyeballs scratched out should the fox not find me as scary as Molly gave me credit for. "I'm coming out," ending the farce.

Shimmying my way free, I began considering a few things. Was Molly making all this up? Was Gus in on it? Who would trap a living creature beneath a bucket and just leave it? And if it was real, what did the fox have to say about the egregious mistreatment?

"Ring a-ding ding," I said in my best Bill Murray, brain mashing the Ylvis lyrics with his Oscar worthy delivery.

"Huh?"

"What does the fox say?" Visions of svelte women danced in my head.

"I *told* you already," Molly said. "He wasn't happy in the slightest."

"And he told you this?" I worried Molly had blown a fuse.

"Well, it was pretty apparent by his actions." She swept her light around the vacant floor we were on. Seventh, I believe. Under construction like four, this was to be apartments. Probably snooty ones.

Something moved. I saw it flash away into shadow.

"There he is!" Molly giddied. "Hello Mr. Fox!" Step after ginger step — the gentle meaning, to be clear — she crept forward toward the edge of illumination. It hid just beyond light's reach. "We're here to help you. Won't you come out?" She crouched.

A noise to the side.

Another behind.

I suddenly had a bad feeling about this.

"Molls, are you *sure* it was a fox?" Because I suddenly wasn't. My stomach lurched.

"Of course! It had a big bushy tail and it was fast." She crept closer to the shadow cast. "A blur of red."

"Lots of things are red," I said. "Foxes. Hats. Blood."

More noises from the shadows. Red eyes and laughter. Holy shit. My heart pounded. Screaming in my head.

"Time to go."

Molly protested. I didn't care. I grabbed her by the waist and tossed her over my shoulder, making for the stairs. I didn't trust the elevator to be fast enough.

She screamed, seeing what came behind. My choice confirmed, I blasted through the stairwell door, taking two or three at a time. "Go faster! Faster! FASTER!"

Sunbeam glared in the lobby, arms crossed and lips pursed, ready to unleash an epic tongue lashing. She stood next to a man I presumed to be Sam. The badge kind of gave it away.

I handed him the previously purloined clipboard complete with check sheet, hardly stopping to say: "Second floor is fine. Three needs the hallways cleared — not even close to thirty-six inches. The Bunker she's going to ask you about isn't worth the sex — sorry, Sunbeam. Don't go up to seven, it's loose."

And I left. Their faces slack.

To this day, I don't know what Molly saw as I snatched her away. She won't talk about it and I won't ask.

Larry's Not-a-Taco

EVERY BODY IN MY bones creaked — wait, let me try that again — every bone in my body — that's better. I'd almost just left it — creaked.

Things were a jamble inside. Bits poking other, softer bits that I didn't think were supposed to ever meet. It had been a tight squeeze getting out of the bunker and then...well let's just say I never want to run this body that hard again. Humans are not light to carry, even once she stopped struggling and realized the need.

I sipped my tea. Walking to clear my brain.

Molly hadn't answered the phone this morning. Or texted to chide me for calling like a savage — as she does. Apparently phones aren't for talking anymore.

Not that I blamed her silence. She'd been confronted with something I can only guess at. I didn't look back. I knew better. There's some things you just don't do and one of them is look back.

Molly had seen the bumps in the night. I worried...

That was odd. Why *did* I worry? About Molly? Very un-me. I enjoyed her company, but she was the one tagging along. I never asked. I didn't know...

"Great shirt, man," said dude with purple glasses. "Sage advice."

I looked down to see exactly what shirt I wore that elicited the comment. It read 'Write Drunk. Edit Sober.'

"Thanks," I said politely. I'd thrown it on at random from the pile. Hemingway, I think. "Nice..." My eyes searched him, looking for a compliment to return. "Watch." You don't see many of those anymore.

"Was my grandfather's." He shook out his arm to check the time. "Stole it off a fellow on Wall Street back in 1978, he said. Light touch." Odd admission.

I kept walking, sipping my tea to distance myself from distraction.

Distraction followed. The thief's descendent caught up to me at the next crosswalk. He smiled. I continued being polite. He looked like he was about to say something. The walking man started flashing go and I went.

"It's only right twice," he said at the next crossing. Determined to talk.

"What?"

"The watch," he said. "It's broken." He held it up to his ear to see if by chance it had resumed ticking.

"Why do you wear a broken watch?" I couldn't help myself. *Beep boop.* We crossed together.

"I like it." No other reason given.

I was surprised he hadn't offered to sell it to me for a good price. Or...

"I'm not going to ask you for money." I wish people would stop doing that. Even if they were gimmies.

"Street magician then?" I patted various pockets to see if dude had inherited the light touch.

He laughed large. One of those rock you where you stand, double over laughs that end in a coughing fit. People stared.

"You're alright," he said. I doubted that. "Haven't had a good laugh in a while." I doubted *he* was alright.

"Thanks." Polite again. Why? I just wanted to be alone with my thoughts.

"You know…" he began, only to be interrupted by the brring of his phone. Guess some people still talked. He held up a finger to take the call. "Hello?"

I took my chance to escape, turning to cross at the next walk. Dude stopped to talk. Thank goodness.

I made a few twists and turns at random to get lost again in thought. People everywhere stared into their phones as they walked about, somehow not running into each other, but only just. Hylic like the rest. The world was in a spuddle.

Molly was different. I wasn't quite sure how though. After our chance encounter at Mallorey's that odd day, she'd latched on. Dangerous addiction.

Her choice though why I worried…

"Seems we're going the same way," dude derailed the train yet again. Case hitched up on his back now. Too small to be a guitar.

"Seems so." I gritted. I wasn't going anywhere in particular. Not volunteering that though.

"What do you write?" Dead set on conversation. I hated that question. Not that I liked any questions. Molly didn't ask questions, though she probably should for her own safety. Too…I don't know

"Bit of this, bit of that," I said. "Just noodle with words really." Vaguer the better.

"Right on brother." Presumed relationship. "I write a bit myself, nothing fancy," he volunteered. " I mostly noodle on this," he patted the case. "Talk a bit, maybe you'll get some inspiration." Dude was persistent.

"Look," I began to disengage. "If I should write you into my stories you should either be flattered or fearful."

"I'd be flattered. Buy you a taco?" He stopped at the hot dog cart we passed. "Could use a bite." Stubborn, this one.

I'd only been a restaurateur for the one day but I knew the difference between a taco and a hot dog.

"What?"

"I see you've never heard of the Cube Rule of Food my friend. Give me two all the way." The former to me, the latter to Larry, the hot dog cart proprietor. I liked it when people wore name tags. So helpful.

"Okay, the what?" I was actually intrigued. I liked picking up absurd little tidbits and it seemed like dude had those in spades. "Explain."

"You know that age old question 'is a hot dog a sandwich?'" I didn't. "The internet has finally answered it."

"By making it a taco?" Not that I didn't like tacos. I did in fact. What's with people deciding cheese wasn't just cheese and hot dogs were no longer wieners?

"It's all about the location of the starch. Thank you." He paid Larry with cash — keep the change — and kept talking.

I bit into my gratis not-a-taco and listened to the profundity of the internet. For the sake of sanity, I'll just sum it up with: who cares what the internet thinks? Not I. Cheese is cheese after all and this dog is hot. The rest was click-bait.

Like his conversational tactics. Thing about click-bait is, it works. I found myself somehow debating the absurdity of starch locations, the sameness of sauerkraut, et al, TV shows canceled too early or run to ground.

Before I realized it the sun was ducking behind the buildings. My frustrations with myself had released a bit. Strange.

Molly dinged me. She was okay.

"Do you need to get that?" Dude was alright after all. I'd just needed to loosen up.

"In a bit," I said. I knew Molly was at least active and talking to me. I still didn't know what to say to her though. I sat.

Dude sat, too. We watched people passing by. Still stuck in their phones.

"There's something you need to know," I said of a sudden. I still don't know why. But this admitted stranger listened.

"I like knowing things."

"I'm not alright," I said, refuting his earlier assertion. "I'm kind of an asshole. I was trying to duck you earlier." I usually did. Another way Molly was different. She snuck in.

"No secret there, brother, but I like a challenge."

"Sorry, usually better at hiding. I'm worried I've gotten a friend in over her head." Ding.

"Was it your intent?"

"No. It just happened. But things tend to happen around me. Things I can't control." I just had to go with the ebb and flow. Mercy of the universe.

Dude laughed. "Said everybody ever. I'm sure she's an adult capable of making her own decisions."

"But they're so reckless..."

"Still her choice. Who are you to judge?"

"I don't want to get her hurt." Why?

"So don't hurt her." As if it were that simple. "Bad things will likely happen. You can't stop them."

I grunted.

"But so will good things. They always do if you let them."

"I should go." I don't belong here. "Be somewhere else." I don't know why I was laying this all out in front of a stranger.

"That's your choice. If you're afraid, run." He cut to the quick. I always ran. Safer for everyone. I was trouble.

"It's for the best." Ding.

"You don't think that."

"Yes I do." Was best for everyone. I keep telling myself that. Every day.

"You're still here though."

I don't know why. I stretched, seized joints breaking like ice in the tray. It still took some getting used to, but I was feeling more and more human. The longer I stayed, the harder it was to go. Try as I might.

"Maybe you're finally getting comfortable in your skin," the dude who knew me for an afternoon said.

I shivered. Chill breeze rising as the sun set.

"Fall is coming. They'll be here soon," I said.

"Who will?"

"The ginger fairies." It was his turn to be confused. "Every fall they steal the souls of every leaf. It's why they turn red and die."

"That's GREAT!" He laughed doubled again. "I can't wait to read your stories brother. I could never come up with something that creative!"

"It's like you've all been visited by the ginger fairies," I said after a bit. He considered what I'd said. I had been observing the Hylic people still stuck to their phones. "Just a new breed." Ding.

"Maybe you should answer that." His turn to disengage. I wouldn't let him off that easy. By his own logic, he chose this.

"Do you know how the first Polish dictionary defines a horse?" Click-bait laid.

"How?" He bit.

"Everyone knows what a horse is." Things that were once obvious were no longer so. People had forgotten. Lost sight of the obvious.

"I'll keep that in mind." Dude puzzled over my cryptic remarks. "But you need to talk to your friend. It seems you've come to a conclusion."

"I have, actually." While I wasn't even looking. "Thanks for listening," I said genuinely.

"Sure thing, brother." He grabbed his case and got up.

"Felix," I said, holding out my hand. "Felix Chance."

Molly had been asking where I was, she wanted to meet up. Somehow I'd ended up at the bench we'd shared after high tailing it from Mallorey's. I waited for her.

She tossed a dollar in dude's case as she passed, having set up busking down the block beneath a purple street light they hadn't gotten around to replacing. Sweet sounds of the ukulele drifted toward me, carrying her along.

"There you are!" She sported a t-shirt that read 'Hide and Seek Champion' with the outline of Bigfoot.

"I could say the same about you," I eyed her. She'd shut herself away for a bit, but apparently was no worse for the wear. In fact, she seemed re-enthused.

"Fell down a rabbit hole," she said by way of explanation. I suppose she'd gone looking for the bumps in the night on one of her apps.

Inside a coil unwound a bit more. I was glad to see her untainted. I'd made my decision.

"I gotta hit the road for a bit." The year was wearing on. I should go.

"Road trip! I call shotgun," she said. Chipper as ever.

"You want to come?"

"Duhhh," she drug it out.

Brow furrowed, I considered it a second and shrugged. I hadn't offered, but also had no right to stop her. At least I could look after her. She *was* an adult.

"Why not?" I looked at her shirt. "Maybe I'll introduce you to ol' Sassy-pants himself."

What's In a Dream of Flesh?

I WAS A MIGHT bewildered.

We needed to get to the bridge before five o'clock when it closed to the island. But the car idly strolling along ahead of us on the bendy road through the trees didn't seem to know that.

Wait. Enraged. That's the right word.

I was a might enraged, not bewildered.

It was a supposedly lovely island with semi-private beaches and dolphins and somehow there were moose as well. They can swim, you know? Moose. Dolphins, too, but naturally you already knew they can swim. What kind of dolphin can't swim?

Skeleton trees on the island, too. I hoped there was some fog. Fog would make them super eerie. I'd wake up early before the sun rose to take a lovely picture. Sit out on the beach and write as the world spoke to me. It would be brilliant and I would be brilliant and produce some finely crafted words.

If this lollygagger got a move on anyway. Who tows a rack of yellow canoes with a 1975 two-tone turd brown station wagon?

"I love this hair," Molly said in the seat next to me. It was purple. Very purple and curly. She admired it in the visor vanity.

"Needs to relax a bit," I said, noting the excessive frizz qualities the new hair exhibited.

Her head jerked back in the seat as I floored it. The gagger was done lollying and had pulled to the side. Huzzah. Luckily the road was arrow straight from here to the bridge. Maybe they stopped to look at swimming moose? I'd see them on the beach, thank you very much.

"*You* need to relax a little bit," Molly said behind me. "The island isn't going anywhere." She brushed her newly purple hair. Like she was calming a cat. I thought. "Hello, yes, I'm here."

Molly had been on the phone for the last two hours of our drive. Rather, she'd been on hold the last two hours of our drive.

Beep-boop. Her phone dropped dead.

In response Molly let down the driver side window and let it fly, the wind whipping strands of lightly lavender hair in her face.

"Island's closed," the pikeman said. That's what you call the people who run turnpikes, right? His shiny helmet blinded me a moment as it glinted in the still high sun.

"But it's not 5:00 yet!" I protested this absurdity. It was only 4:57. I had three whole minutes to spare and by gods old and new, I was going to get them.

"By the time you get there it'll be 5:00 not to mention we have to leave room for people coming back. The boat can only hold so many."

"Fine, I'll just wait here then." I could have made it, I didn't add.

Instead, I sat my baggage down in the terminal. All nine suitcases and a hat box. I came prepared. I was nearly at five hundred words so I took out my tiny typewriter and pecked at the keys. Others filled in the ferry terminal as I sat against the grimy window coated in sea spray and noticed that somehow a spider had gotten in between the two panes of glass and built a web.

I waved at it. It waved back. Or maybe it was building a web.

What was even more remarkable was that it actually had bugs in its web. How? Was there a micro-ecosystem of bugs shifting through the glass molecules just to be eaten by the spider in the vacuum?

That would suck.

The toaster dinged. Molly was yucking it up with our fellow would-be passengers of the boat that had never come. My cinnamon bagel was done. Very fragrant, reminding me of the fields in which they grew.

"Oh I just love your green hair!" The wind had calmed it a fair bit. Was that what a blow out was? Stick your head out a car window and voila, that'll be seventy-five dollars please.

"Thank you, it's really growing on me." She coifed her blue locks as the strands began swirling and twining around her fingers, growing thicker. Healthier. She said she was using a new conditioner, guess it was working.

The tea bag twirled as I watched. First one way, winding itself up on the string, then the other.

Mesmerizing. Hypnotic almost.

It never seemed to slow down.

Wind.

Unwind.

Wind.

Unwind.

Drip. Drip.

It dripped and dripped and dripped until I grabbed the scalding hot bag between my fingers and squeezed out every last drop. Don't waste good tea.

The hours waned as the night grew long. We couldn't decide what movie to watch as the red headed gate agent joined us in our vigil. She was cute, if mildly infuriating.

Every time one started, we'd be interrupted by something or other and never get very far. I couldn't seem to focus on what was playing anyway. I just remember a flash of Christopher Walken's face. Or was it Christopher Lloyd.

He wore glasses on his head. Like, on top of his head, not the bridge of his nose. Like Molly's sunglasses threaded through her hair. It was longer still now. Covering most of her face down past her shoulders. She'd tried to put it in braids to keep from tangling in her sleep.

"Your teeth look sleepy," she told me before she vanished beneath silver threads.

Why would my teeth be sleepy? They were perfectly happy in my mouth, relishing in the delight of tiny bubbles as I brushed to fight the plaque away. Ahhhh. Refreshing. Ting.

Outside the moon grew dark. I was running late and I hurriedly threw on some books and ran down the stairs passing a fox flying about.

"Hey, watch it!" The fox yelled as I overtook him. Revving my engine like an asshole. I couldn't be late again. It shook its red fist at me.

Couldn't be late. Couldn't be late. My feet were lead and would not move, try as I might, they just wouldn't move.

"Can't move from here, we'll be spotted," I told my girlfriend. She was new. I can't remember her face too well.

She didn't want her boss to see and he inconveniently lived two streets down in the same neighborhood. I needed a distraction.

We were pinned down and they wouldn't send help. Somehow I knew it was because he also didn't want to be spotted. Or I didn't.

"Why'd you come here," I asked Dominique, one of my lieutenants, as she came through the secret tunnel. "You'll give me away!"

I'd done so much to hide my evil organization in this unassuming little town and she was going to wreck years and years of hard work. I just couldn't believe it. It was unfathomable. Everything spiraling red down the drain.

"I seem to have forgotten how a dryer works," Molly said, mostly hair now. She tried to blow it from her face. "At what point do I set it on fire?"

"I think you're supposed to set it one step short of fire," I said, confident in my answer. She had laundry she'd wanted for the beach trip.

In the terminal again, it was hot as we waited. I sat watching the redhead as she laughed with the others also waiting for the boat. She'd been off duty for hours now. Could have gone home at any time. But still she remained. Why? She laughed and caught me out the corner of her eye.

Dawn was breaking. She swayed over and gave me a smile. I think she wanted to kiss me. So I kissed her on the cheek and slipped away — before she could say anything she would regret, or I would — leaving my luggage behind.

"It's four to six," she called after me. "You've almost made it." I could see the Lorelei rising from the water over the horizon.

"I know." And left just before it was due.

"Is there a point to this?" Molly sat listening. Cheek resting on hand.

"There's always a point to dreams, even when there's not." I sipped my tea.

"Is *that* how it works?" She checked her hair. Not purple or green or blue.

"Sure," I said. I'd been talking nonsense for two hours now. Some was bound to slip in.

The Doyle Museum

CONNECTION. FEW THINGS MATTER more to an artist than this. To be able to transcend space and time through some vestige of their soul imbued in their work. That simple meeting of hearts when an art lover or avid reader discovers that one special thing.

It's why so many get taken advantage of by offers of *exposure*.

"Son of a bitch," Molly said.

And why I now stood behind a velvet rope at the Doyle Museum.

We stood before an oil painting of a particularly frozen pond, Molly and I, connecting with the artist. Now gone.

"Told you," I grinned. And I had. The title of the piece was, unironically, *Spring's First Blush*. "It changes with the season."

"Says here it's called *Frigid Morn* though," Molly read the incorrect plaque. "Artist Unknown. Acquisition Unknown." She looked at me.

"I knew her," I said, a bit hollow and low. Damn sneaking grief. "And that's just what they call it this stop." No one around. I snagged a quick selfie with the painting for my records. Fake title plaque and all. They couldn't well call it by the proper title when the pond froze over and the trees donned their white, could they?

I'd shown Molly the others. Me, in front of the painting showing the same small pond, the same tree growing out of the same oddly shaped boulder. The only compositional element that changed was sometimes there was a guy fishing and sometimes not. His inclusion and activity depended on the day of the week.

"We come back tomorrow, he'll have a bonfire blazing." I knew the schedule well.

Molly leaned over the stanchion ropes as far as she could to get a closer look. Maybe trying to see it move. It wouldn't, not when you were looking.

"Is it a TV? Some kind of fancy e-ink technology? NFT?" She'd stepped to the side to see if she could spot glare or some other inconsistency in the surface. I knew all she'd see were the fine strokes of the brush on stretched linen.

I knew because the painting belonged to me. Once.

The work of one dearly departed. Her most overt. A gift for me.

But she deserved to be in a museum. To be adored through time. Cherished by people other than myself. So I made the connection.

It's pretty easy really, there's a simple trick.

You see, museum security is pretty much focused on preventing people taking art out, not bringing it in.

Ahem. A pointed throat clearing from the guard. "Three feet back, please."

"Sorry, bad eyes," Molly squinted at the guard. The guard squinted back at her. I tucked my phone away. No photography please.

We moved on.

"Oh they know," I told Molly at the Shake Shack. I munched on some fries. She slurped a shake.

"Are there dozens they swap out after hours?" Molly couldn't fathom. Trying to figure out how the trick was done.

"Nope." My turn to slurp.

"It changes. When no one's looking."

"Yep."

"How?"

"Who knows?" She knew. She who made it. Who once held my heart and holds it still. I only knew a bit of the how, and I wasn't telling.

I hadn't told *everything*, just enough to stoke the flames of curiosity. Molly didn't know the provenance. Or that I'd been the one to slip it in this traveling exhibit — a bunch of paintings depicting myths and legends from across the pond. Fitting home, I thought.

It had been a gamble, and I won big.

I had no idea it'd actually get included with the collection. For sure, I thought that even if they didn't notice its addition tucked in the corner — with a proper frame and title plaque to match all the rest so as to blend it in — while the show hung, that surely they would notice the extra when they crated it all up for the next stop.

No one did.

At least, not that they admit. Like they don't admit the scene changes every night. Like they don't admit why the exhibit moves cities every three months — when the differences become too stark. Or that they purposefully criss-cross the map in order to escape rumor. Like they don't admit they're scared of its sudden and inexplicable appearance and are too afraid to *not* take it with them for fear of it just showing up again.

Plus it *was* quite lovely.

Talk spread. I'd heard the guards at every stop. *That one, the haunted painting? Gives me the creeps.* or *Did you see? The leaves all went from green to red!* They tried to keep a hush on it, but word got out.

Which had formed the basis of the urban legend I now plied Molly with.

Ever since the Byron encounter, she'd been drawn to the paranormal — ghost stories, cryptids, the occult, anything *other*. If there was a subreddit for it, she was in. It's a fairly common reaction, in my experience.

Otherwise, you tended toward madness.

I was like a candle to her moth. Things tend to happen around me. If Molly was going to continue being close, I had to be more careful to keep the flame away.

But I needed her help.

Once in a great while, one special scene appears. I needed to be there for it. Alone.

"You're some kind of something." I don't know why I said it. She cocked her head and quirked her nose at me.

"Is that supposed to be a compliment?" Slurp.

"Yes."

"Thanks." She smiled.

"You're welcome." I'd run out of things to say.

"You're stalling." I was. "Out with it." She pointed at me with a fry stolen from my plate. Chomp.

I sighed. "You remember how I covered you while you got your jollies at the Byron?"

"I remember how I literally saved your and your little tart's — what'd you call her? Sunshine?"

"Sunbeam. And that's not..."

"Sun*beam*'s ass in the shelter." Molly cut me off. "But yes. We both got something out of that." She didn't mention the not-a-fox. "What about it?"

"I need a favor."

"Sure." She stole more fries from my plate.

"Just like that?" I was surprised.

"For real, we're friends, Felix." She laughed as if it were the most simple thing in the world. "We've been through a fair bit now. Besides." She paused, making sure I had her full attention. "Fun things happen around you."

I knew the feverish look in her eyes. Hoo boy.

Three days later.

I'd confirmed it was the right day. The bonfire had burned for two straight nights. Right on schedule. I had to be in front of the painting right as the sun set.

The plan couldn't be simpler. I would make my way through the museum and Molly would...well... be Molly.

I hadn't just been buttering her up when I said she was something. She was. Strange things may *happen* around me, but she *makes* them happen. She created impossibilities.

Like the ginormous bearded moose currently trotting through the abstract expressionism gallery to the screams and clattering feet of everyone in the museum. I wondered briefly if its tastes lay more with the realists before fighting the urge to flee. Despite my dream, I was not mentally prepared for a moose.

"Run! Run! Run for your lives!" Molly yelled, waving patrons out through the exits. "There's a moose on the loose!" The fake panic in her voice was belied by the belly laugh attempting to burst from her face. I think the moose scoffed as it shuffled through the halls, care given to its massive antlers.

The museum was small and the moose was large. And where moose are universally well known to be assholes, this giant with silvering forelocks was respectful. Wisdom glinted in his black eyes. I suppose only the young bucks are the assholes.

Asshole or not, his presence was more than enough distraction. Everyone had fled in short order. Guests, guards, gawkers — gone. Molly locked the doors behind them. The moose thwatted the cameras with its antlers.

We stood before *Spring's First Blush*, the three of us. Myself. Molly. The moose, whose beard she amiably scratched. The scene the same as before — the pond thick with ice — however, there was no figure fishing or doing any of the other routine activities. No. Instead it was empty. Quiet. Waiting. Footprints had formed in the snow.

"Where'd you find a moose?" Breaking the silence.

"I gave him a pumpkin and asked him nicely," Molly sidestepped the question.

"You asked him nicely?" The moose — a good eight feet tall — nodded his massive head. Yes.

"And to also not hurt the art," she said. He snorted as if to say 'like you had to ask.' "He said he'd be very careful."

"Thank you," I said, addressing the moose. He lowered his eyes a fraction, respect earned. To Molly: "Thank you." I'd been tempted to press for more answers, but didn't.

I have my secrets, seems she has her own. Only fair.

The sun dipped low and I glanced down at my watch. Antsy. Nervous. Sunset on the Solstice. It would happen then.

"Let's check out the impressionists," Molly said to the moose. She'd sensed my tension.

Alone now, the painting came to life before my eyes. Daylight turned to night as the sun set. Both within and without. Out marched a wedding party mounting the boulder's crest to stand beneath the tree. The branches of the massive tree reached towards the heavens, illuminated with thousands of candles this night. A mimicry and mirror of the countless stars that had been in the sky.

I watched as the bride and groom stood before a robed figure with a beatific face. His face toward me, theirs away. I could not hear the ceremonial words or the blessings or the joyous music playing through the air, but I knew every one of them by heart. I remembered them well.

They turned.

Suddenly I flashed before the bride, lifting her veil for the kiss. Her face glistened with joyous tears as we wed. She was all I saw, she who held my heart. The world fell away, but it mattered not so long as we were together.

"I love you," she mouthed as our lips drew close.

"And I love you..." I said in memory, my voice catching at her name.

And it was gone.

She was gone. The sweet warmth of her lips left only to memory. And to this moment eternalized.

The sun had set full and she'd left me yet again. Alone. I wept.

I wept not for the empty ache left behind, she would not have wanted that, but for the happiness and joy we shared. For the stolen moments when we could just be us, together. Where I was okay, made whole.

The guards, newly armed with tranquilizer darts and a big net — one had a riot shield— broke down the door and filled the room.

Inside they found no moose. No Molly. No me.

Only a vacant spot on the wall where none would admit my wedding gift had hung.

Maya

I KEEP SEEING PEOPLE linger in the corner of my eye. The face that's not there smiles at me in memory.

The rain had been uncalled for. Sudden steam sussing from the streets and sidewalks filled the air, dampening sight and distorting sound. Helping the mind to play tricks. Painting the grey with errant memory.

I was on my way to see Molly. She'd found a building she fancied and wanted a wingman to intercept the inevitable. As I walked, the ghosts formed around me in the fog. Dim bubbles of blue illumination bursting in and out on the city street as people checked their phones to confirm that it had indeed rained. Their faces lost. They paid me no mind.

I lurched forward, my toe catching a crack or a curb unseen. Disorienting. I could not even see the hand in front of my face. Such was the fog that I began to doubt I even had one.

I slowed my pace and, seeing as there was nothing to see here, drifted. Bagpipes echoed in the distance, strangely twisted. A Williams score. Thankfully the piper did not play *Amazing Grace* — the vibe was funereal enough.

I don't like it here. It pulls at me. Tugs at my edges. Every time I'm in this place it hurts, taking away a little more of me. Here charm is strange and strange is charm, at least that's how I made nonsense of it.

Honk. A distant horn that seemed somehow bent. For me? I wondered. Sound baffled like cotton in my ears. Honk Honk. A train trundled past.

I recalled fog like this before. Thick as pea soup children's books call it. Vaguely I recalled Levar reading that into the camera. *Abiyoyo* was probably my favorite then. Or at least the one that stuck with me. Take a look.

Back to the fog. The fog I remember had happened when they took my forest away. It had been hot that day like today and the lumbermen came to clear the downed woods. We couldn't afford to do it properly, it was just too much. Too much damage from the ice, to my father, to me. And the forest was old. It would soon burn had we done nothing. I knew. Dread.

They came with their saws and their hatchets and it rained. Rained hard for a mere twenty minutes, but it was enough. As they cut the woods, the fog seeped through and among the trunks. Tendrils stroking the mossy earth as if in consolation.

And the forest was gone. I felt it gone. Like the spirit leaves the body at death. Bereft. Part of my home slipped beyond. I cried.

My stomach turned and twisted. Walking in seeming nothingness.

"OW, damn it!" I barked my shin on a bench in my stumble. "Lucky me."

I felt my way along the edge and sat down. It was senseless to go on. Time for a good sit. I'd wait it out.

Intentionally thinking nothing takes great skill. Skill I do not possess. I'll spare you the sordid details, but suffice it to say...well, nevermind.

It was time for me to go. The building I was destined for would be obvious, she'd said. Right at the intersection of five streets. A good old flatiron.

I knew Molly was going to be pissed-angry. Or pissed-drunk. Maybe horny. But I think pissed-angry was most likely.

"A mix, but mostly pissed. Still am." Molly interrupted as I tried to explain how I met a ghost.

"The fog cleared the streets leaving no one." Picking up. Mood I'd been setting shattered.

"Maybe they all fled the rain," Molly considered. "Sensible thing to do. But it was still a dick move to ghost me."

I sighed. The irony. I couldn't. I have trouble with it myself.

"I tried," I said instead. I had stood staring in her face and called. Nothing got through.

At first I thought she was purposefully ignoring me. Pretending I didn't exist. Molly could be angry all she wanted. I was in a mood myself. Memories I didn't want. Places I didn't want to be. Let her huff.

I had been supposed to meet her at the cafe on floor one and work our way up through the flatiron's interior to the sky top bar on floor twelve, exploring the preserved details of yesteryear as we went.

It was a lovely building, I must admit. I could see why Molly fancied it. The fifth floor was brilliant. Straight out of a Bogey flick. Doors with frosted window panes. Office numbers and names painted on the glass in gold. I was slightly disappointed none of them had been for a detective agency. Missed opportunity right there.

Also no Molly so I kept working my way up the labyrinthine floors. You could walk your way up to the top whilst never using the elevator or actual stairwells. No one impeded my progress through the building. Deserted though it felt, the flatiron was not empty. Footsteps echoed. Snatches of bagpipes again reached my ear, drifting through the corridors. Perhaps the piper had an office here.

"Did you see the barber chair?" Molly lit up, momentarily forgetting she was mad at me. "And the typewriter nook? They worked! People were leaving messages on them, and..." She resumed her cold scowl. "I can't believe you explored without me."

"Well I didn't exactly linger," I said in my defense. "I was looking for you in the very you places I thought you'd be."

"But I wasn't." Molly huffed.

"No, no you were not," I said. Molly had been at the bar, more precisely on the fire escape that served as the city overlook, rubbing up against the wrought iron railings.

I tried to catch her eye as I worked my way across the crowded space. Nothing. People bumped me left and right. Oblivious. Drunk. Assholes. Something. I wanted to shout 'make a hole,' but it would have been lost to the din.

"Buy a girl a drink," I said at last, finally making it to her. She turned away.

"Look, I'm sorry I was late." I moved back into her line of sight. "There was this crazy fog and..." Ignored.

Molly walked away.

She slipped easily through the crowd that entirely obstructed my attempt to follow. Ducking through a window, she vanished from my sight.

"I had to pee," she explained, looking slightly nervous as she did.

"I figured, when you came out of the bathroom and stared me straight in the face." And through me.

"I did not!" A bit on edge are we?

"Then why'd you pause *right* in front of my face, not a foot away?"

"I..." she hesitated. Was this all some confabulation? An elaborate ruse to mess with me? "I heard something," she finally said.

"What?" I thought I knew, but wanted to see if she said it.

"I heard crying," she said. "Like it was coming from inside the bathroom with me." A smile.

It had. Right as Molly stared through me, before the bathroom door could close, a woman in a red cocktail dress ran out. Tears streamed down her face as she bolted for the window. Then screamed.

The piper played it this time: *Amazing Grace*. Loud. Ear-burstingly loud. I turned and there stood a green haired goth bedecked in rattly chains climbing towards piercings in her pale face wailing on the bagpipes. Marching forward into the crowd, she bumped into me.

"Excuse me," I said. I opened my mouth to ask a question now lost to time. Thought cut short when the piper turned, shocked, the bag went poof.

"You can see me?" Her painted eyebrows raised higher than their already unnatural arch. "You can hear me!?" She grabbed my shoulders and shook. "You feel that?!"

"Woah, woah, lady," I brushed her off. She stepped back with her clomping, stomping boots. "Yes I can do all those things. Why the hell are you blaring the bagpipes while red dressed girls run crying from bathrooms? What kind of bar is this?"

"Don't mind her," she said of the lady in red. "She does that all the time. Drama queen." She scoffed.

"Who are you calling a drama queen?" She suddenly changed. Green gave way to alluring raven curls. Her eyes smoldered as shadow spread across her lids and red lipstick kissed her face. She screamed again as fishnets fell into the scarlet dress brushing the floor. The very picture of a fatale movie star. "Relax, dude. It's part of the act."

She flourished with jazz hands and vanished.

"And it worked!" She appeared right behind me, scaring the bejeezus out of me. "You can see me!" She spun and launched fireworks from her fingertips. Sparklers maybe. "You can seeeee meeee," she swooned, her eyes locked on mine. A peculiar shade of gold.

"Yes." I stepped away, again. "I can see you. And hear you. And feel you." I confirmed all of these things of which she seemed in doubt. "Is that so unusual? You're pretty hard to miss."

She waved a feathery white fan in front of her face. "Why yes," she said. "It is actually." She thwapped a passerby with the fan. He kept walking. "See?"

Odd. The bar kept bustling around us. No one gave a second look to the sparkling showgirl standing next to me. Or to me.

"Are you a ghost," I asked the presumed ghost. I added things up quickly. "Am I a ghost?" I patted myself, checking for damage. Perhaps she would know, being the resident expert on ghosts. It would explain why Molly acted like I wasn't even there.

"Not a ghost," said the still presumed ghost. "Just stuck this side of perception." She poked me. "Did you die? I think that's a prerequisite for ghosthood."

"I don't think I did," I said. I'd have felt it, right? There'd been the fog and the noises, but I certainly didn't remember dying.

"Neither did I," she said, seeming less like a ghost now. "I just seem to be stuck here."

"Where is here?"

"Hell if I know." Glasses and a lab coat appeared. "Maybe some other dimension, split off from our reality? Different by a couple molecular twists? I don't know." She shrugged into a sweater. "I thought I was alone until just now."

"Excuse me." I held up a finger to think. Pacing. Processing. I tried to remember what I'd had to eat that day to see if the list included anything hallucinogenic. How was she doing the clothes thing? That bit tickled my fancy. She'd said it was part of the act. Was all of this an act?

I turned to look for Molly and found her at a corner high top surveying the room, occasionally swatting away bar flies buzzing about her with unhygienic offers. I'd confront her and suss out the truth.

"This is absolutely remarkable!" I swept my hands at the crowd that carried on acting like nothing was happening. "How'd you get all these people to go along?" Nothing. I got right in her face.

"She can't hear you." From behind again. A little to the left. My turn to do the ignoring.

"Is this a friend of yours?" I hooked my thumb over my shoulder.

No comment.

I called Molly's number while I looked her in the eye. The phone didn't ring. "Doesn't prove anything. She keeps it silenced." Most did these days.

"See?"

"I need a drink." I made for the bar before I thought better about it, then turned and grabbed a whisky from a white-haired gentleman with wild, frizzy hair and, for some reason, mutton chops. "No one will ever believe you," I said unheard.

"I *don't* believe you." Molly's arms were crossed as she stared at me.

I shrugged. "It happened."

She shot me a side eye. "Then how'd you get out?" Piqued curiosity laced through her voice.

"Just lucky I guess." I winked at Molly.

And at Maya, smiling, perched on the chair behind.

Beckett's Bar

FIRST, I WAS DRUNK. I want to make that clear.

I don't get drunk often, rather hard to get me drunk in fact, but Damian was buying and he's the generous sort. Very generous. Buys for the bar.

It all started with a bet, as most good stories do. The stakes were high. I had to win. So I did the best thing I knew how. I cheated.

A little bit anyway.

"People forget I'm kind of awesome," I said. I forget that myself, most of the time on purpose. Bourbon loosens the tongue as much as it helps to forget though, and a loose tongue remembers many things.

Like my encounter with 'squach.

Luckily most dismiss it as a bar story. Reminiscent of a fishing story that grows larger and wilder with every telling — and every drink — but no trout were harmed in the making of this tale. But sometimes...

"I'm telling you, Bigfoot likes his beer."

"And you would know?"

"Yes." I nodded resolutely. From my former life. "I've seen proof."

"Oh? Show us!"

"I can't. It broke the computer." It had. Video proof and nothing would read the disc. Even got stuck in my friend's MacBook. Wouldn't spit it out for a couple months. Then one day — Pop — out it came. Scratched all to hell.

"Sure sure." Damian ordered another round. Laid down another bill.

"For real." Why I felt I had to defend my word here — *needed* to be believed — I have no idea. I lie for a living. Beautiful truths they may be, but still lies. "These Bigfoot hunters showed me the video and burned it to disc." I spread my hands to show it was gone. "Disc was a coaster." Highly disappointing and marginally creepy. Little did I know then.

"What'd you see?" Molly was intrigued. I hadn't told her this one before.

"Pretty standard shaky cam to start with. Night vision stuff. Trail cams with shadows. Sounds."

"So nothing..." Damian didn't believe. No amount of tequila would change that.

"Wait...that was just the beginning. I was skeptical, too." Was my job to be. "But then, clear as day. Big hairy behemoth walking upright through the woods carrying a keg like you would a beer." I poked his chest for emphasis. "Five more slung over his shoulder."

"Bullshit." This from another guy.

"Gods' honest truth," I held up three fingers. Maybe two. I wasn't sure how many by that point. "Spotted somewhere between a college and a nuclear plant." That had been comforting.

"Tell 'em to come drink here," the owner of Beckett's Bar laughed. "You'd buy for Bigfoot, wouldn't you Damian?"

"Damn straight!" Another round, another bill on the bar. "If he existed," Damian smirked.

"I'll prove it," I shot my mouth off. Real smart.

And so we find ourselves riding down the highway, Molly driving the T-bird, me with the window rolled down and a large steaming coffee to sober me up.

Damian and his bar buds close behind, no doubt with a full bottle of Patron. I preferred whisky myself, but I needed my wits about me now.

"Where are we even going?"

"*The lake* of course. The one from your manual." I intended it as a joke. It did not play as such.

"Seriously, Felix, I know he threw down ten grand, but why do we have to literally go to the middle of no and where?"

"You wanted to meet Sassy-pants, too," I said.

"Can't we con him out of the cash somewhere with AC..." Molly was a bit grumbly and a bit skeptical. Strange things might happen around me but there were limits to the suspension of her disbelief.

"Not a con." I'd told her I'd introduce her, and I make good on my word. Even to doubters. I closed my eyes and leaned back, shoving the spinning world away.

We stopped at the requisite sketchy gas station. Still had a *Pure* sign on it. As well as a rusted old 'For Sale' sign propped up against chipping white cladding. Glad I didn't have to piss, the bathroom door was padlocked. Wasn't sure if that was to keep customers out, or keep whatever bred there in.

Damian, though, he'd had a few more than me on the night.

Donnie, the station attendant with the ever helpful name tag, gave him the key which dangled from the end of a two-by-four cutoff. "Careful in there, youngun, don't wanna fall in. Gators might getcha!" He laughed, his wizened face crinkled with amusement. I could almost hear his leathery skin creak.

I pumped our gas and peeled off a couple of bills.

"What's for sale," I asked, nodding toward the sign, its spikes stained muddy red, as if it had just been pulled up.

"The sign," Donnie hooted. "Ten dollars!"

"Pass," I said. "Got any beer? Maybe some coolers and ice?"

"Lake trip, eh?" He squinted at me and our ad hoc, unprepared crew. "I got ya covered. C'mere." He led me in through the screen door and time stood still. This place was from an era well and truly gone.

Grime covered every surface, only wiped away in the places often touched. Those spots were well polished. Bottles from sodas lined the wall. Glass ones, long emptied. Tins for other items joined them. I grabbed a few cases of beer from next to the live bait stand and Donnie pulled out a styrofoam cooler.

"Gonna need a few more than that," I said, going back for a couple more cases.

"Long weekend?" He eyed me.

"Expecting a thirsty guest," I said. "Any kegs?" I doubted it.

His eyebrow shot a bit higher and reached for two more coolers.

"And these," Molly said, sneaking up behind. She dumped an armful of chocolate, marshmallows, and graham crackers on the counter.

"No kegs, ice out back," Donnie hooked his thumb attaway as he added up the tab.

"Thanks," I grabbed the beer and coolers. "He's paying for it," I nodded to a queasy Damian bringing back the key.

"Never use the bathroom," I grinned at his sour expression. "It's in the manual."

"Didn't you drink enough last night?" Molly hadn't partook nearly as much as we had, which is why she now drove. I sensed slight disapproval.

"Bait." I simply said. "Sassy-pants likes his beer, remember?"

"Why do you keep calling Bigfoot Sassy-pants?"

"You'll see." She drove on, her face a grimace squinting into the setting sun.

The woods around the nuclear plant were prime real estate for ol' Sassy-pants. No one wanted to live there. Peacefullike. Idyllic if you didn't mind the rads. And there were always drunk college kids to steal beer from.

Tonight it'd be freely given though.

"So what's the plan?"

"Well, it's like this, you see," I drew her in close. Conspiratorial. "We crack open a few beers." I did.

"Right. Uh huh." She looked over at Damian's crew fumbling with sticks for a fire.

"And wait." I took a sip to demonstrate.

"..for Damian to get super drunk and then scare him with the suit you snuck in the back when none of us were looking?" Her eyes hopeful.

"No. Just wait." I handed her a beer of her own. We had plenty. "Don't worry."

She threw her hands up in exasperation. Ye of little faith.

"I'm going to look so good behind the wheel of that T-bird of your's, Felix." Damian mimed cruising around in my ride. "Well, soon to be mine." He tossed an arm around me. "I gotta say I admire your cajones man, sticking to your guns like this."

"Always do sober what you said you'd do drunk," I replied. Another Hemingway.

"That's good man," he laughed. "I like that! Respect." He grabbed a six-pack and headed for his boys. They'd come to make sure we didn't welch on the bet. I had until dawn to produce.

Good news though, I was going to get ten grand out of Damian. Sassy-pants would come through for me. I cracked open the bait. Time to wait.

Waiting sucks. Especially when it's hot as balls out, as it currently was. Molly had insisted on a fire though, so I sat well back as she made her s'mores.

Molly being Molly, she served them to squirrels. Seriously. They chattered at the edge of the fire's light, beady eyes glistening in the flames. Waiting. Waiting to dart in and snag the stupid humans' food.

Instead, she slid the gooey treats off the sticks she'd stuck up by the fire to roast the marshmallows and sauntered over to the little squirrels waiting by the bush. They darted back and forth. Ducking for cover then coming back out as she drew closer, enticed by the sweet smells and Molly's sweeter presence.

"Come on little ones, I'm not going to hurt you," she cooed, then made some chittering sound of her own. "I've got some super delicious s'mores for you!" And she dropped a piece near the bush.

One brave little squirrel darted out to grab it back to the shadows. Another poked its head out to distract as a third nipped up from the side to grab a bite fallen to the ground when she'd broken the other bit. Clever lad.

Molly laughed sweetly at their antics and broke off bites for them as they gathered 'round. One let her pet its fluffy tail, likely her goal in this whole endeavor.

We all sat transfixed watching the exchange, Molly glowing by the fire's light. When came a crash of branches from deeper in the woods. A knock and a snort.

I shot to my feet and I flicked on my flashlight. Damian grabbed for a branch and tried to stand, toppling back to his rear — he'd gotten into the bait.

"Damn son, it worked!" Damian waved a fire log the direction of the sound.

It grew louder, larger, as something *big* was making its way through the darkened trees. Deep in the night, home of things that go bump.

"Elder!" Molly squeaked in delight upon seeing our friend the moose come through the copse and into the camp's circle of light. He snorted hello.

"Chill guys," I said. "He's a friend." I put myself between the bewildered drunks and the giant moose.

"Have you been swimming?" Molly slung water from where she'd tried to pet him. The moose — Elder she'd called him — dripped as he stepped closer. "Come on, let's get you a beer."

"Moose like beer?" I knew he liked pumpkins. For some reason I pictured maple syrup too. But not beer.

"Oh they love it!" Molly all glee as Elder energetically nodded, slinging water over the rest of us. "No s'mores for you though," she chided as she dipped into our diminishing Bigfoot bait to share with the moose.

The fire grew low as Molly regaled the group with the tale of Elder in the museum — the parts she knew — with the moose weighing in where appropriate. I watched the whole scene unfold to store in my memories.

Bright, sparkling ray of hope. Good hearted, boisterous adventure seekers — they weren't getting my T-bird though. Squirrels unnamed darting too and fro, nibbling discarded

bits of treats. And an Elder of the Forest settling in for a
hazy summer nap after a dip in the lake — he took up half
the camp by himself.

It's quiet now as I write this. Only swarming bugs left
for company. Grown fat and large on humidity and human
blood. Blech, I think one got in my mouth. Thick as the
air I currently wear. I always hated that line, but it makes
sense now that I cannot abide even a single thread of cotton
touching my skin. I couldn't sleep so I wrote all night. It was
time to put a few things down.

The night is dark and the dawn is far, but in this I find myself
and share. Words upon words flow from my fingers as the
night clicks away.

Come the dawn, now not far, camp stirred. Elder had left
well earlier in the eve, after Molly dozed off but before all
the beer was gone. Damian awoke and stood in a hole for a
second before remembering the rest of the night before.

"Bro, you talk big, but man do you swing it!" Damian
dropped a fat envelope in my hand, avoiding looking down.
"Damn son."

"Just remember that," I winked and pointed the cash at him
before tucking it away. "Next time!" I called after him. He
turned and waved, back to reality.

"Put some clothes on!" Molly threw a shirt at me.

"Too sticky," I complained, dropping the envelope as the
cloth hit my face.

Molly caught it and looked inside. Her jaw slacked.

"Wait...what?" She looked up to me then over to Damian
and his boys driving off, not in my Thunderbird. "You won?
How?"

"Check your phone." She'd been so excited to meet him,
she wore herself out before he even showed. So I snapped
a selfie. Molly, me, and ol' Sassy-pants.

"For what?" She flipped her phone around. "Just pictures of you and me and your thumb."

Well damn.

Index

PRECISELY TYPED ON THE three by five was this address:

```
Saffron School for Confidence
     One Twenty Shaw Street
        Pembreton Oaks
```

The meticulous care with which it was typed quite evident in the even strikes of the letters, the strict alignment of the lines and peculiar spelling out of the street number.

I had received the card the night before.

A strange encounter to be sure. I wasn't quite sure I would in fact find the address.

It's surprising what you can Google these days.

> What is the airspeed of a coconut laden swallow?
> African or European?
> How is Amanda Palmer's friend Anthony?
> Sadness awaits you.
> What is the third door on the right from my house?
> Your neighbor.

But Google was flummoxed when I enquired about the Saffron School for Confidence.

A small round man had given me the neat little card. He was entirely fascinated by them, bordering on obsessive. He seemed to have an index card for every occasion and scenario likely encountered. He'd had a parrot, as well, most suspiciously. It kept asking the same question over and over again: "How's ya boy?" When asked about his card fetish, the round man simply replied: "They work, you'll see."

I could use some confidence. I thought. Maybe. Okay definitely.

I walked with imbalance, not yet adjusted to my new body. As a once fat man does when he has lost significant weight. Swaying. Stumbling. Overcorrecting for a load no longer there.

It is difficult to break years of reflexive action at sudden change.

It was one of these overcorrections that led me to the small round man with the squawking parrot on his head. Yes, his head. It was hard to talk to the man because you didn't know whether to look at him or the bird.

It was slightly disconcerting for t'was the bird at eye level.

At any rate I'd been walking along and stumbled on a broken paver when I braced too hard for the accustomed weight shift, no longer present, causing me to lurch back the opposite way grabbing the scaffolding against which the short round man was vaping. His parrot flapping wings in the clouds streaming from the holes of his face like a deformed and somewhat hairy dragon poser.

He doffed his black bowler hat, upsetting the parrot though not dislodging it from its perch. "How's ya boy?"

"Fine thanks, sorry about that mate. Still getting used to the body."

I'd responded to the parrot. The round man said. "No worries, down here chap." He waved.

"Right, sorry."

I was fidgety, new body and all. Not used to the bits and jobbers.

"Lost? Abandoned? Need help finding something?" He asked and pocketed an index card.

"No, just clumsily totting about. Seeing what's what."

"Well the what's what is Shirley's Good Time Review, wings and tits galore," the short round man said, pocketing another card. He peeked another and smiled an awkward smile.

"I'll keep that in mind." Stepping back.

"You look a proper chap though so maybe Harvey's Wine & Dine Power Bar, catering to the l33tiest of l33ts since two thousand aught seven." Another card.

Nervous.

The short round man consulted his concealed stash of index cards yet again, picking several. "How's ya boy?" Nodded and stepped closer in attempted camaraderie.

"Look, I've never been able to tell anybody this, but I trust you. Implicitly," the man began reading from his card, "and I've not felt this way in a very, very long time," stepping closer. Uncomfortable. "I have the," pause to change cards. "Consumption. Wait..." confusion as he flips through cards. "Ah!" He finds the card and holds it out at a distance. "Secret to Happiness. And want you to have it too."

The man handed me the three by five and said nothing more. He turned and walked. A final "How's ya boy?" from the parrot the only words in parting.

Now I was here on Shaw Street in Pembreton Oaks looking for number one-twenty and not finding it.

"Just a twist and a step and whaddya get..." she said, appearing on thin air.

Not from thin air as if I simply hadn't noticed her being there, no. On thin air. She stood a good seven inches above the ground on which I stood, her, on apparent nothingness.

"Oh, hello," she smiled and held out her hand for me to assist her descent.

I obliged out of habit. Providing support as she delicately stepped down beside me.

"My you're tall, hmm," she said upon reaching the ground. Then she stepped back up to her original platform to look me almost in the eye. "That's better."

"How are you..."

"Well thanks, and yourself?"

I'd been going to say 'doing that?' before she interrupted. Impertinent sort, she was. This silver haired girl standing — er, floating? — before me.

"Still getting used to things," I said, stretching my back in ripples.

"Stop that, you're tall enough!" She stood on tip-toe to gain some more height. Apparently I'd been growing.

"I'm a little lost," I said instead, flashing her the index card with the absent address. "I'm not from here."

"I know. You're from that side of other," she said it as if it were terribly passé. "I've seen your sort before." She took the card from me. "What's your name?"

"I'm Jake," I tasted the name. It was new to me too.

"No you're not," she denied me. "Terrible name. You need a better one."

"Yes I am." Brilliant counter.

"You don't look like you're from State Farm." She eyed me up and down. "Where's your khakis?"

"In my other pants." I tried to be a smartass.

"The khaki ones?" She smirked, one hand on her hip. "Look, we can either stand here and debate your pants and the terribleness of your name or you can come inside."

"It's not terrible," I sulked.

"Give it up love, they've ruined it for you. Come on then," she turned on her heel and stepped.

From behind me, a sudden shove. As if she'd gone the wrong side round to give me a startle.

It worked, too. I'd spun round, tripped on my own feet, and fell ass first into wherever this was.

Where before there was a gaping hole in the storefronts — skipping right from one-nineteen to two-twenty-seven down the block — now sat twin revolving doors spinning opposite ways.

"Who are you," I asked, getting up and brushing myself off.

"My name's Helena," she said, though I somehow doubted, "and this is the Saffron School for Confidence." She swept her arm over the letters engraved in the building facade. They did not read the supposed school name.

She led me forward toward the spinning double doors.

"Mind how you go," she said as we entered the left.

"Don't want it to hit you," she said, coming back out the right, "on your way out."

The intervening time is still a blur. Seconds. Days. Years. I hadn't the foggiest.

What I did know was more about myself than I ever wanted to, a bit of cocky added to my swagger, and that the world was a many strange and wondrous place.

"Everything else will come as you need it," not-likely-Helena with the silver hair said with a wave of her hand. "Now, have you finally picked a better name for yourself than Jake?"

She looked at me expectantly. I tried to recall all my lessons, blurred in half dreams. I hoped to find something that tasted right. That spoke to the strange quirked bits of fate which had taken hold.

"I think I have," I said, rolling it around in my brain. "Call me Felix," I said.

She tasted it herself for a moment, failing to come up with any snide remarks. Maybe Felix passed the sniff test. She smiled.

"By chance, I happen to like it," she approved.

"Chance, huh?" I appended the last name on the first. "I like it!"

I waltzed down the street and with a step and a twist, I was back on Shaw. Noise assaulted me the moment I did, crowded clamoring noise from the city and the crowds and my own belly.

"I could go for some soup," I said. The rest fading from thought.

Achoo.

Bunny

I DON'T KNOW WHERE this story starts, or where it ends, so I'll just start telling it.

Maybe I should start with this guy called St Germain. Or maybe pigeon guy. Nah, rewind a bit more to picking up Bunny on the outskirts of Vegas. Always offer the lady a ride. Especially when she asks so nicely.

"Drive Drive Drive Drive," she screamed, hopping in the T-Bird's passenger seat, shoving a gun up my nose.

It was a little peashooter of a .22, but at close range, that'd still do. I shifted into gear.

"I said DRIVE!" Hysterics full bore, she climbed across, half in my seat, and stomped the gas. The engine revved louder as we crawled to a halt.

"What are you doing?" She looked around, panicked. I fought to keep a straight face as the lunatic with the gun just kept pressing the gas. Going nowhere fast. She'd knocked the T-bird out of gear.

Men came out of the motel across the street. Two of them. One limped, the other pulled yet another gun — this one not a peashooter — and pointed it in my general direction.

Two guns pulled on me in as many minutes. Super. Not off to a great start here. I didn't know who she was or who was after her, but I liked my chances better not being stuck in the middle. No lead had yet flown and I wanted to keep it that way.

I shoved her out of my seat, off the shifter, and put the T-bird back in gear. Dust kicked up as I hightailed it out of the gas station lot.

Neither gun fired — hers wouldn't, spent. This improved our relationship slightly.

But only slightly as she still held her little pearl handle Derringer in my face.

"Put that down," I said testily. "It's entirely impolite to point."

"Why should I?" Her wrist twinged a little as she pointed it harder for emphasis. "No, just drive." She looked at the empty road behind us then back to me. Then back to the road. And me.

"Your wrist must be killing you," I said.

"Just, like, drive okay?"

"I'm driving, see?" I floored it, shifting up a gear. She lurched back, swaying unsteadily in the seat.

More vigorous pointing. "I don't want to shoot you!"

"You're not going to shoot me." My tone was quite confident. This woman was scared and a touch angry. I don't know what sort of trouble she was in, didn't care to either. I'm not one to pry. But I needed to establish some civility between us or this would get real old, real fast.

"I shot them!" She waved her other hand back the way we came. "I can shoot you, too!" Desperation.

"Yes, you shot them. Twice," I said. "And good for you!" I tried for affirmation. "Though your second missed."

"How?" Her face worked slack. Pretty face. A blonde, not fake. She was trying to follow.

"Your wrist is killing you right now," I said gently. "You can put it down," I said. "I know it's empty."

"But..." She looked at me. Then the gun. Then lowered the gun. She sighed.

"Besides, you can't work a stick." I shifted for emphasis.

"Maybe not that kind." Bunny shot me a wicked look.

"Where ya headed?" I changed the subject. "You never said."

"Wherever you are," she said, propping her feet up on the dash. "I needs a nap."

Either she just didn't care anymore, her tense energy spent, or I'd instilled some trust by continuing to drive.

We rolled on through the desert. Bunny sat shotgun, a touch more calm. Dozing peacefully. No one had followed. No dust cloud beside our own.

How do I always get stuck in this stuff? I shouldn't even be going to Vegas, but I got a letter. Honest to goodness wax seal. Neat, flowing hand. Even an illumination of the sort monks used. A majestic lion rampant to the right, all done in green ink with flecks of gold.

I'd found the letter by chance, slid under the door of a place I was staying. It had been addressed to a name I had once owned. No envelope, no stamp, no sender noted. Delivered by carrier pigeon, I was left to presume.

The letter had simply requested the pleasure of my company. No time. No place. So I ran. I ran to hide among the hylic. Lose myself in the desert away from those I now knew.

Nothing for miles on either side. Not even a cactus. I expected to have seen a roadrunner, or at least a coyote shaped hole. Just my current copilot, still unknown to me.

"Most guys'ld've tried something by now," she said. To illustrate her point, Bunny grabbed her chest — among various other lewd or suggestive gestures. She had quite the repertoire.

"I'm a gentleman."

"There's nothing gentle about you," Bunny said. She cast an appraising eye over me — one used to sizing guys up. "But you're respectful," she nodded. I wasn't quite sure how to take that, but I suppose that was enough to put her at ease.

Signs of life sprang from the desert, desolate still. Downtrodden at the edge, worn. In the distance the oasis that was Vegas sprouted like a pimple on the flat, tan skin of earth. Gaudy blemish.

I drove along, making turns at random. I'd never been before and my navigator gave no guidance. We rolled down Fremont — I'd at least heard of that — heading downtown. Old Vegas, I've heard no local call it — it's the tourist name — just call it downtown. Or Fremont. The lights weren't on yet, the sparkles glinting only in the beating sun. Damn it was hot.

"You can leave me here," Bunny said. She'd stirred and apparently spied a suitable destination. "Thanks for the lift," she said as she got out. "And for not, you know," she pointed a finger gun at me, "taking it personal." She leaned in through the window and pulled down her top, flashing me as payment for the ride.

A memory I fully embraced as I sat in my cell awaiting...well I wasn't quite sure what. I don't recall ever being arrested before. Who knew you could get nicked for punching a pigeon?

Nice and round, still pert, but they didn't look done up — no hard silicone lumps masquerading there, not like Sunbeam. Large enough to be fake though. Bouncy. Barbell piercing through one, holding on a shiny stainless shield. Blue butterfly perched atop inked ivy, slightly grayed, which vined its way down through her cleavage leading...

Stupid pigeon interrupting my fantasies. Ought to punch him again in his stupid plastic pigeon face. I hate it when those damn stupid memories intrude. The bad ones. The not-too-proud moments of anger that just get seared into the prefrontal cortex. Just when you've calmed down and are totally not thinking about them anymore they just pop in for a spot of tea.

I felt my blood pressure rising again.

Traveler's tip: Anyone doing anything on the street considers themselves an entertainer in Vegas and expects to get paid for even looking at them, it seems.

Pigeon guy was sitting on the street in the middle of a flock of — you guessed it — pigeons, feeding them bits of bread and scattering seeds, wearing a giant rubber pigeon mask over his head. The flock consumed him. Hopped all over his outstretched hands. Pooping all over.

Why the mask? He was trying to blend in? Holdover from Covid? Dysfunctional furry fetish? No.

My guess — based on thorough psychological examination and careful observation — is the anonymity to be an asshole. Like on the internet, but in real life.

Cousin of yours? I'd texted Molly a shot of the absurdity and leaned up against a rail awaiting a reply. The three little dots danced on my screen — Molly's one of those texters guaranteed to reply quickly, obsessively che—

SLAM-jangle

"Hey!" I look up from the bucket of coins making the clangor to see the pigeon mask up close and personal. "Pay me, jackass!" He shook the bucket again for emphasis. Still in my face.

"What?" Despite its age and wear, the mask retained that new latex smell. This somewhat pleasant smell was obliterated by the raging breath of the guy demanding change. I stepped back.

"You took a picture!" His tirade continued, pressing forward. "You take picture, you pay!" Deranged. His eyes dangerous.

"Listen pal," I said. "I'm not giving you any money."

"You pay!" He shook his bucket at me again. "I perform, you pay." He nodded as if this was known.

"Just because you put on a stupid mask and make a fool of yourself doesn't make you a street performer," I said, stepping around him to leave. "That's not how it works." I knew how it worked. I'd been there. Fog thinned on memories of sidewalk busking.

Before I could follow that cognitive trail, he took a swing at me.

You don't take a swing at me. That much did slip out of the fog. Many options of varying finality presented themselves to me. I'd tried to walk away...

I ducked the poorly aimed hook and came back with an upper. He sprawled backward over the pavement, his bucket rattling away — change spilling everywhere.

Threat down. Efficient.

And in seconds, I too was down and cuffed. Punching pigeons man. Who knew?

"Punching pigeons, really?" A slim man in bespeckled black echoed my thought as he approached my cell bars. "How uncouth," he laughed. Trim white hair, dressed neatly, with diamonds pricking light from the darkness. One in his ear. A stud set in his collar and each of his cuffs. At his throat a purple cravat.

"You again?" I wouldn't give him the satisfaction of asking how he got back here — he delighted far too much in explaining his magnificence. Instead: "Leave me be."

He laughed.

"That won't work on me." Cryptic much? I had no idea what that meant and before I could even suppress the quirk of an eyebrow his words flowed on. "I do like a captive audience."

Probably the only ones that listened. I'd made the mistake of sharing a blackjack table with him shortly prior to the pigeon punching and barely escaped then. I remained silent.

"Why you haven't yet walked out of here, I cannot fathom." It gave me the creeps. He seemed to know things about me, things I remembered only in dream. That, or he was great at cold reads.

"Tends to raise some eyebrows," I said noncommittally. I made a show of stretching and being comfortable. Didn't quite work. I'd been sitting too long and so, instead of smooth nonchalance, my foot flopped about fish-like.

"So let them be raised." He waved a dismissive hand, the sickly fluorescent light glinted off his pinky ring. Square gold set with, you guessed it, three diamonds, small and round. A few flourishes worked their way out either side down to the band.

"I'm not like you," I said to the Count of St Germain. That's how he'd introduced himself. At great length. Many, many words fell from his mouth in rapid succession. He'd gone on to make several outlandish claims about his title and personage and grandiloquent exploits over the past several centuries.

"Dear boy." St Germain exhaled a sigh and shook his head. "Still?"

That's right, I said centuries. Apparently he's an immortal alchemist.

Did I mention that?

The Count of St Germain

I'D TAKEN HIS MEASURE at the table, but it'd cost quite a bit.

When I'm counting a table, I prefer not to be seen. Not to be remembered. This 'immortal alchemist' — I use quotes because, really? — defied all attempts at anonymity. Weren't they supposed to work in secret?

"Quite the place you've chosen," St Germain had said, approaching my table with a lovely lady on each arm. Dressed well and entirely unfamiliar to me.

"Have we met?" I knew we had not, but he came directly to my table like he knew me. And what did he mean by 'chosen'?

"A lifetime ago," he said, "but as you wish." He proceeded to talk as if we were simply catching up after an extended absence. He did so in an infuriatingly grandiose manner which any attempt to recreate I made would pale in comparison. Suffice it to say, it was entirely pretentious and grating. You're welcome for the omission.

The count was at four — the cards, not St Germain. He was at seat six — a number I kept repeating to myself the entirety of the Count's reintroduction. He really made it hard to focus.

Dealer had an Ace, I had a King-eight. Stand.

"A nine and a three? What garbage is this," the Count said. "Hit me."

King. Bust.

"Of all the luck," St Germain said. "Can you believe this?" He asked me as he waved at his cards. "Trade you that eight for my nine."

"Don't think it works like that," I said. The dealer smirked. Don't be memorable. Don't be memorable.

Dealer flipped a seven. Push for me. Count cooling down to a two, but that's doable.

"What do you think I should do?" The Count puzzled over a six and an eight. Stand on the dealer's two, obviously.

Honey, the amber haired tart on his left had another strategy and said "Hit me!" After which she giggled. I think she'd been drinking.

"Oh!" Sunny, the platinum one on his right said, "I wanna be spanked, too." And proceeded to lean into the Count.

"Later, sweetheart, I assure you," the Count said in a growl and gave her a squeeze.

A third chippy, raven haired, joined St Germain from behind, bringing champagne for the other two. She draped herself across his back, resting her assets on his shoulders and began kissing his ear.

"Quite the Casanova," I couldn't help but remark. His little harem giggled.

"My dear," he said. His gaze landed on me, the ripe lasciviousness dripped from the words as the world narrowed to him. "I'm far superior to that ignorant slut."

I broke the gaze and laughed.

"Oh that's right!" Time for distraction. "I totally forgot you were immortal! So you knew him then?" I slowly raised my bet.

"I did indeed, the braggadocious upstart. Half the tales Giacomo told were co-opted from my own, trying to pass mine off as his," the Count was certainly incensed. "After all I taught..." He cut himself off and smoothed his expression. Hurt and betrayal had seemed to play across his face.

St Germain withdrew from his pocket a finely worked leather and glass flask containing within a liquid the color of Honey's hair. The elixir seemed to glow in the glitz of the room. It might have been a trick of the light, but the glow seemed to come from within.

By that time a redheaded stunner joined the party. It seemed our dealer had started to drool a little. Guess she liked gingers. Distracted dealers are great and all, but not when they draw over the boss.

More cards flipped. All of them low. Ridiculously low, pushing the count up to seven. Dangerous with the pit boss circling, but I had to play my game. I raised my bet.

"You seem to have found some confidence in your play," St Germain said to me. He leaned back and thumbed out seven chips of his own. "I'll follow suit," he said and tossed them in.

Damnit, don't call attention to it! I thought. My face hid a scowl. "Feeling lucky I guess," I said instead. "It's nice when the lady smiles." Make it look like I was a degenerate gambler. Casinos love those.

Counters not so much.

St Germain got a blackjack, suited no less. King-Ace of Spades.

"I'd have preferred diamonds," he said to Ginger on his lap.

"Diamonds are pretty," she tittered.

"And so are you, my dear," he kissed her playfully.

"We've come to bring you luck," Honey said from behind. When had she gotten there?

I turned and she wrapped her arms around my neck, kissing me deeply. I felt hands on my chest as she did. Then my legs. Too many hands. Raven had joined and turned my head.

Intoxicating. They were everything I hated. Everything I wanted. To lose myself again. The perfect punishment as I gave in to their lips.

"Sir," the dealer coughed. Twice. I looked down to see a blackjack of my own.

"There's more than that," St Germain said. "Should you come back."

Back? I laughed nervously, pretending confusion. Inside, my stomach dropped. Something screamed to flee.

"Shall we go?" He'd said it then and he said it again.

Before, I'd denied him, gathering my chips and cashing out.

Now, I waved my hands at the intervening bars. I still felt the caress of temptation on my body.

"My dear, I've talked my way out of beheadings before," St Germain said dismissively. "Talking the constibliary out of misdemeanor charges is no harder than breathing."

"I don't need any favors from you," I said carefully. Slightly testy — I was tired. Favors were dangerous. Especially from anyone claiming to be an immortal. That tread dangerous territory, actual alchemist or not. Best to play it safe.

"Besides, it was clearly self-defense," St Germain carried on as if I hadn't spoken. A habit that was quickly becoming annoying.

"You were there?" Had he been following me? Had one of his tarts? Seen using other means? It would explain how he even knew I was here.

"No no, but it's all over TikTok." St Germain held out his phone. "You're viral!" I entirely expected his case to put even Liberace to shame. Instead, sleek slick metal formed seamlessly around the device. Metal the like of which I couldn't place. The dull glint of it tickled something...

"There's even a charming remix," he said, tapping through various videos setting the incident side-by-side with singers and musicians and people reacting. Playing it forwards and backwards. My head replaced with various meme faces. Great.

"I'll never hear the end of this." Molly would make sure of that. She'd be all over this if she found it — and she would, it was on an app. She has all the apps. I bet my phone was already blowing up in that little baggy they'd shoved all my confiscated belongings in.

"Coming?" St Germain cocked his head and swept a gracious arm toward the exit.

"Nah. I'll take my chances." I kicked back and propped my feet up again. No favors asked or accepted. I did not want to get involved. Not with him. "Like you said, it was obviously self-defense."

The Count's inviting expression dropped, face becoming unreadable, elegant hand flattened to his side. Cold.

"Do you ever tire of doing things the hard way?" The way he spoke intimated a familiarity that rankled me.

I shrugged. He wasn't wrong, by any stretch, but I had no inkling of who the count was and so was reluctant to take him into any sort of confidence.

"A small word of advice: always let them get a hit on you, dear boy, then it's battery for them instead of simple assault.

Sticks better." He flashed a wicked row of white teeth. "Especially if you slip a knife in their... pants."

"I'll remember that." Substitute 'back' for 'pants.' I closed my eyes, inviting the Count of St Germain to take his leave.

I replayed my recent encounters with the purportedly immortal alchemist — strangely familiar and yet entirely alien. The way he spoke. The things he knew — especially about me — he had no apparent way to. Unnerving.

I'd thought it best to keep a discreet eye on St Germain.

After he lost his taste for losing at my former table, I'd seen him crash the one hundred and first birthday party of a lovely lady by the name of Ethel.

Now Ethel was spicy for one hundred and one. You'd never know it from looking at her, but she had a handy sash — consider it an upgraded name tag — proclaiming both her name and status as birthday girl. She and her crew of sexa-, septua-, and octogenarians, plus caretakers, had taken over a row of slots into which they fed coins.

No one could get in or out, blockaded by wheelchairs and walkers as it was, but somehow St Germain had managed the feat.

"A toast!" The rowdy clutch of little old ladies surrounding the birthday girl cheered the new come ebullience. St Germain certainly had a way with people. Taking them into close confidence moments after meeting them. The same presumed familiarity that grated me seemed to work wonders on others. The Count poured Ethel a toast from his own flask, the one I'd seen him discreetly nip between hands earlier.

"May you spend your days in good company and taste the joys of a life extraordinaire, my dear Ethel."

"Cheers!" They drank the toast, Ethel imbibing the amber elixir St Germain had poured in her glass. Her eyes sparkled as she did. I felt radiance suffuse her spirit, a golden warm glow spreading throughout. She clutched the Count by the arm.

"My my, young man," she laughed. "You remind me of this wonderful gentle soul who I went steady with a few years before the war." Age fell from her face as she spoke, standing taller as she gazed up into his face. "You could be his grandson."

I saw her transported as she spoke, back to the days of her youthful giddiness at this handsome fellow paying her court back in the days when people did such things. Why does no one court anymore? It's all wham-bam hookups. St Germain smiled in fond memory as well, his eyes alight with seemingly shared memory.

"Why my dear Ethel, that was I who shyly gave you that clutch of daisies," the Count said. She laughed at the idea, mirth cutting through the years. "I plucked them from along the roadside as I walked to your farm, counting myself most fortunate to find them!"

"Oh you kidder," she patted his arm. "That was more than eighty years ago. When I was a young thing." The crowd around tittered at the idea. The count was a hit.

"Why yes, you had the most darling braid! You loved to coil upon your head, I do recall," St Germain said, stroking her starkly pink hair, dyed for the occasion I presumed — because when you're a hundred and one you can do whatever the fuck you want — cut close to the scalp. "It was much longer then," he said. "And chestnut brown. But I certainly approve of the new do." He winked.

Tears sprang to her eyes. Her mouth wordlessly worked, trying to find purchase. He leaned and kissed her cheek, whispering something to her before departing.

This Count of St Germain spoke openly about things as should be kept to hushed rooms, and while he seemed to be full of it, there was just enough credence to underpin his preposterous claims.

Now I was doubly glad I hadn't invited Molly along on this little expedition. I needed some time to sort myself after all these memories kept bubbling through the thick layers of fog blanketing my brain. The questions that would follow her meeting the Count with his overt declarations, I'd have no answers for.

I'd had none for my own.

The bars of my cage rattled open. I'd drifted in my reminiscence. It must be well past nightfall now. Despite being dead tired, having driven for hours and then hijacked at spent gunpoint, I couldn't truly sleep.

"Chance," the guard called. He'd been none too gentle booking me earlier. Usually someone buys me dinner first before heading down there. O'Mally, his name tag read. So stiff, formal, the last name tags. I vastly prefer to be on a first name basis. "Judge set the fine at six hundred," he said, sounding slightly disappointed. "Can you pay?" The glint in his eye said he hoped I could not. Maybe he was lonely working the midnight shift. Wanted someone to talk to. Sure, that was it.

"That I can," I said as I threw my feet to the ground to stand. "It's in that bag with my other stuff."

O'Mally grumbled as he undid the door lock, letting me out of the holding cell. Still oddly empty. Must be a slow night in Vegas. "Come on," he said.

I retrieved my things and bid adieu, hoping to never see the inside of one of those again. (Spoiler, I would, but not this trip.) My phone dead, likely drained from the incessant texts and general shittyness of the battery — maybe I should chuck the whole thing in the Bellagio fountain and be done with it. No, it was too far to walk. Besides, they'd frown on that and I'd hate to make a return trip so quick.

For this reason, I strictly ignored all of the street performers vying for my attention as I made my way down the street.

Also because I was broke.

My fine was exactly the amount I'd taken from the tables before the count turned sour.

I chuckled.

And so I was left with my dead phone, the rubber band formerly securing a wad of cash, and apparently a comp pass to a dinner show that had not previously been in my belongings. Must have slipped in by chance.

Lucky me. They were having tacos — of the not-a-hot dog variety, don't worry. I don't think the Cube Rule of Food has corrupted Vegas yet.

The Freaks were out on Fremont. A clown juggled as I passed, careful not to make eye contact. Same with the red-feathered showgirl and three card monte hustler.

Lady was on the left. I was tempted to try my luck against his slight. I resisted and moved on when a dumbass picked the one in the middle — it's never in the middle. Good luck, fool.

A slight girl folded herself into a box. I'd stared too long — a kid, maybe her brother, son? — made a move toward me with a hat. I moved on, ducking behind a fat guy with a yardstick, his belly hanging out of his shirt.

Never make eye contact. Eye contact invites involvement. Once you've seen them, they can act. Like many other things.

Some don't take kindly to it either. Especially the ones who don't want to be seen. Like the shadow that slipped behind a flashing neon sign — I tried not to notice — of my destination.

Persephone's Lounge, the sign read. Pink cursive letters surrounded with flowers in bloom. Fitting for the goddess of spring. The triple Xs fit, too.

Gold tassels led to my seat — a front row pass, to my surprise. I was just after the tacos, I lied to myself. I was hungry.

The ladies came out and did a wonderful number. Lively music. Great dancing. The siren headlining the show was mesmerizing. Next table to mine was filled with women of a middling age, one younger than the rest. A niece perhaps? They clapped for the dancing and the singing.

Their food arrived, distracting them from the show. Mine came next. I'd ordered a variety platter that offered a bit of everything — spicy carne asada, fried fish tacos, soft shell and hard.

My eyes traveled up from the food set before me to thank the server. Didn't quite make it all the way up.

My eyes stopped. The pair of tits bouncing in my face were strikingly familiar.

For Want of an Elvis

"I DON'T THINK THEY'RE wearing shirts," one of the sweet ladies said from the table next to me.

Well duh, it was a nude revue. Music, dancing, stripping. All inclusive.

If they'd been wearing shirts, I'd never have seen the blue butterfly bouncing in my face, which belonged to none other than my good friend Bunny.

"We meet again," I said pleasantly enough. "How's the wrist?" I smiled and hoped she didn't pull her .22 — not that she really had anywhere to hide it.

Bunny flipped her hair and straddled my lap. Then she slid her arms back over my shoulders and around my neck, leaning close to whisper in my ear.

"You don't know me," she said low, then gyrated back around, whipping her hair in my face. "Got it?" She thrust her booty in my face and left.

"Oh my," I heard from the table next to me, followed by some hearty laughter. I looked to see the other dancers performing similar moves on these priceless women.

Strange encounter, certainly, now passed, I ate my tacos and thought.

I was exhausted. Mentally, physically, spiritually. All emotion drained, barely putting up a front. Funny how not conducive to rest a jail cell is. I mean, what else is there to do besides sit and wait? Nothing. A raw nothing. It's boring as shit, but there's no turning off.

Empty, anxious energy coursed through my veins. Outwardly, I ate my tacos, but inside was a mess. Like tacos, we all fall apart sometime.

Parts of my brain were apparently off limits. I hadn't really noticed the lack until I really looked for things I should know and found only a mental shrug. And yet there were times of perfect clarity.

This was not one of those times. Things were happening as they always do, by chance. Pure happenstance. Coincidence to the max.

Bunny brought me a drink. Margarita. Perfectly timed companion for the fish taco that was next up on the platter. She bent over to deliver it with the standard sultry gaze. Flirtations included in the price of admission.

I smile my thanks, nothing more. After all, I didn't know her.

Funny that she'd leave me a smeared note on the drink napkin then.

I don't know how you found me or why you came looking, but since you're here, I need a best man.

"Who's wedding?" A very mellifluous voice laced with curiosity disrupted my thoughts. Him again. Great. The Count of St Germain sat down at my table, sans chippies this time, and swiped a taco.

"I don't even know," I said, halfway honest, folding the napkin over in my hand.

"Matters not," he said. "Hardly a better choice, dear boy." Again with the overfamiliarity.

"And you would know?" I shot him a skeptical side eye over the salted rim. "Why are you following me around?" I was tired of the stalker routine.

"What's your game," St Germain said, quite testily. "You ask me to this hylic hell hole and pretend not only that you didn't but that you don't know your own kin?"

Thunderstruck, my mouth slid open agape.

"Invited?" I said dumbly. Kin? I kept to myself, not ready to deal with those implications.

"Indeed." The count smoothly withdrew an invitation, twin to my own, though this one sealed with red, and placed it squarely on the table.

I pulled out my own crumpled invite.

The count frowned, staring at my missive and his as if one or the other were about to bite him.

The music began to pound — or was that my heart? — drowning out thought. Another round of dancers paraded about the room as I tried to consider what was happening. Too many things to be pure chance.

I folded open first my invitation to slide to him, then grabbed his from the table. His bore an illuminated dragon clutching seven coins in taloned hands. Also noted was the precise location, time, and circumstances of our meeting in the same flowing hand that had been so vague for mine.

"What does any of this mean?" I waved my hand over the twin missives. "It's gibberish." He looked at me distantly, almost with a hint of sorrow.

"Gibberish indeed," he said. "You've forgotten the language of birds." St Germain stole my drink for himself, draining half. "And this," he waved his hand at me, "no act?"

"Look," I said. "For the thousand millionth time: I DON'T KNOW YOU."

The music chose then to cut out. Typical. I smiled awkwardly as the room stared at me.

"We have a volunteer!" The PA blurted as mostly naked women surrounded me with feather boas, herding and tugging me up to the stage.

"Hey, wait," I protested, being dragged along. "Hold on." Feathers buffeted my face as the crowd cheered. St Germain simply sat there sipping my drink, watching as I was marched to my fate. I saw him dip a finger in the margarita and wipe it on one of the invitations.

"Round of applause for our daring devil here," the PA continued as I neared the source. "Handsome, isn't he?"

"Woo!" The nice neighbor ladies cheered and called. Hopefully they didn't want me to take it off.

"Stop, I didn't..." I tried to back out as we neared the steps. Soft hands — and other parts — pressed against me, cutting off my retreat.

"Now don't be shy." The guy with the mic and slicked back hair motioned me up on the stage with a sequined arm. His whole jacket, in fact, was covered in them — red and sparkling in the spotlight. "Come on, come on. The show's only an hour long." His dimpled chin wagged as he coaxed. "That's a sport."

Front and center. So much for not drawing attention.

"What's your name, pal?" The emcee held the mic to my face for a half second before yanking it away again. "Great Frank," he said, not bothering to care what my name actually was as he led me to another cone of light. "Now what I want you to do, Frank, is stand right there," he pointed to an X. "Oh Melody," he called off stage.

A blonde — not Bunny — walked out covered in glittery paint that left absolutely nothing to the imagination. The crowd whistled and called as she swayed her way to her mark next to me, rolling a large box on to the stage.

While the audience was distracted, the host dropped the mic and the act for a split second. "Look pal, you're causing a disturbance, shouting and passing notes to my girls. Can't have that." His too white smile turned to grimace. "Plus that sour puss of yours is spoiling the mood here," he finished. I had no time to protest. The show smile flashed back on to his face. "Thank you Melody."

He walked back to the center stage spotlight while Melody, he had called her, opened the box extravagantly. No name tag visible — because where would you pin it on a woman only wearing paint? — so I'd have to take his word for it.

She motioned for me to step up into the tall box. I guess this was the magic portion of the variety show?

VROOM VROOM VROOM VROOOOM

Another beautiful assistant had handed the magician a chainsaw. Spattered and rusty, he revved it with manic glee in his eyes.

"Don't worry, it won't hurt," Melody whispered to me as she locked the doors of the box in place. Not comforting in the slightest.

"Now if you're the squeamish sort," I heard the loon say, muffled by the box.

CLICK

The world fell away. Or maybe it was just the floor.

I landed with an "oof"

"Shhh," Bunny whispered, finger drawn across her lips. "I told you not to know me," she added.

"What in the hell..." I began. She cut me off, her hand over my mouth.

From above the chainsaw revved and made cutting sounds. Sawdust fell on us from above and Bunny screamed.

Loud.

Loud and girly.

"Frank, you sound different," I heard the muffled line from above. "Must've cut a little low." The audience laughed. "Knock twice if you're okay."

That was Bunny's cue. She popped up into the hole I'd fallen through and knocked once then waited a breath before knocking a second time.

"Wait for me in the back," she poked her head back down, nodding toward a small opening. "If you want to be my best man, anyway," Bunny smiled, a wicked glint growing in her eye before she vanished above stage.

"Phew," the magician exhaled loudly. The pause designed for comedic effect. "Okay, now..." he began as I shimmied my way out from under the stage.

It was tight. Secret passages typically aren't made for comfort. I don't know how I know that. It's just one of those clarity things. Go figure.

"Wozerz!" The audience gasped, then laughed. The sounds followed me. "Hell of a upgrade, Frank!"

Boobs everywhere. Of every shape, size, and description. Bouncing, jiggling, glittering, the ladies of the show ran back and forth between outfit changes, makeup touch ups, hair maintenance.

"Excuse me," I said, standing up. "How do I get back to my seat?"

'You don't, hon," a stern looking woman stopped short in her dash. "You come out here, means you were a problem."

"Mhmm," another performer said beside her. "Back door's attaway," she pointed, finger ending in a wicked looking talon of a fingernail. "Git while it's good."

"But she said to wait for her," I said, kind of lamely.

"Who did?" Suspicious, both of them.

I hesitated. I didn't actually know Bunny's name — she never told me. This is why I like name tags damnit, so I don't keep making up lame nicknames for the people I meet.

"I didn't catch her name," I said instead. "The woman I swapped with." I motioned vaguely back under the stage and scratched the back of my head. I thought about adding that she'd asked me to be her best man — whatever that was about, maybe it'd add validity to my claim — but thought better of it since Bunny's best man ought to know her real, actual name. So instead I just kind of smiled and chuckled.

Awkward. All of it.

"You can wait by the door," the first one said.

"There's a chair right on the other side with your name on it," the other said, hand on hip.

I took the hint.

Outside, the wind rose and gusted in my face. The promised chair was no longer there, likely carried away by the oncoming storm. I spat dust from my mouth. Flashes in the distance lit the sky, thunder rolling in long after, almost lost in the city noise. Almost.

I hoped Bunny hurried up. I did not want to get rained on in the middle of the desert.

Maybe it was a dry thunder? If it's a dry heat in the desert, other things can be dry whatevers, too. Not one accompanied by rain.

The door swung open with a bang. Thunder to the lightning flash of Bunny, stepping out in blinding white. Head to toe, she gleamed in a well-cut tux. Lacy, sheer white veil trailing behind.

"Well," Bunny struck a pose in her wedding whites. "Fab, isn't it?" Who knew a tuxedo could curve like that? It swayed as she walked. I hurried after.

"The wedding's today!?" Though, I guess it was tomorrow already. It seemed like so long ago that she'd held me up with her .22.

"We're eloping," Bunny squeed. "Have to be hush hush about it," she said. "Her daddy doesn't approve." She made a face somewhere between lemon and thunderhead.

"Hard to imagine," I said, a touch more drily than intended. The storm rumbled on, more distant, rain threat abating.

"Look," she snapped. Was she always this tightly wound? "If you're going to be an ass about a girl marrying a girl, I don't want to hear it." She sped up to leave me behind.

"Wait, no. Sorry." I stopped her and rubbed my tired eyes. "It's been a long day that started yesterday," I said, trying to explain. "Or was it two days ago?" I couldn't remember at this point when I'd gotten the letter and vamoosed. "Anyway, seven hour drive. Got hijacked at a gas station."

"I said sorry," Bunny pouted. I shot her a look before going on.

"Ran some tables, punched a pigeon," I began reflecting on the absurdity of it all, "for which I got picked up, culminating in being kicked out of a titty bar before I could finish my tacos."

"Busy day," she nodded.

"Z," I added. "Busy days. So no, no problems with the direction you swing. I'm down. She's a lucky lady," I smiled.

"I'm the lucky one," she skipped a hop as we walked. Pep in her step I didn't feel myself. "Oh!" Bunny fumbled in her bag, suddenly remembering something. I saw her flash a wad of cash, which I quickly covered.

"Do you want to get mugged?" I said it low and close. "What are you doing walking around with that kinda cash?"

"Eloping," she said by way of explanation. "I picked up an extra swing tonight just to pad it out. Good tippers, too." Her face lit with a smile. "Besides, I reloaded. Here," she held out the piece of paper she'd been hunting.

"What's this?" I took the folded paper.

"Your grocery list? Drink recipe? I don't know," Bunny shrugged. "You left it at the table," she said. "You're welcome," she brightened.

"Thanks," I said, slowly. The only paper I'd left at the table was the invitation, and this was not it. Maybe St Germain had left this for me? I carefully unfolded the note.

Know me or don't, I well know you, dear boy, the note read. As you seem to no longer know your own self, allow me to provide a remedy... the note went on listing off ingredients I could barely decipher. I'd have to wait until we stopped to read it more carefully. Make some sense of it.

"Bay leaves? We fancy," Bunny read, catching a glimpse over my shoulder. "What kinda drink's that recipe for?"

"I can't remember, exactly." Along with the ingredients, there were instructions. "Did you read it?" I held it up for her.

"Just the last part," Bunny scrunched up her nose. "The rest is gibberish. You have terrible handwriting."

Strange. Not my hand, but I could read it just fine.

My thanks for the missives, St Germain finished up. So he did take them. Together they provide the key to what I seek.

Maybe he saw something where I had not. A mystery for another day.

For now, Bunny and I were off to find a black-market Elvis.

Bonus — House Painter

DENNY'S IS WHERE YOU go to hire a house painter at three o'clock in the morning. Apparently.

At least that's what the nervous woman who approached me thought.

"E-excuse me, sir," she said. She looked fragile. Slight frame in mom jeans and a cardigan buttoned over a white blouse. "Do-do you paint houses?"

This last she whispered while looking around to see if anyone watched. An odd question to ask a stranger tucking into his Grand Slam at 3am to be sure. When I learned just exactly what she wanted, well I looked back at my eighth grade science and social studies teachers a little differently. They'd told the class once they painted houses to make a little extra money over summer breaks.

For the moment though, I was clueless. And broke.

"Yes?" I replied with a big question mark and a definite upturn in my voice.

"Oh good, I'm in the right place," she said, relief evident in her voice. "This is the first time I've ever done anything like this, and I pray to God it's the last, but I just can't stand living there anymore."

"Okay," I said, thinking it a bit dramatic of her.

"I can't sleep, I can't eat, that place is ruining my life," she said a bit unhinged, lighting up a cigarette. She certainly seemed like she hadn't slept in a while. Jittery was an understatement and she carried the sleepless nights under her eyes. How many did it take to cause those suitcases?

"And so you want me to paint your house?" I was uncertain that a fresh coat of paint would do much good for her psychological well-being, but she seemed to think it would and I needed the money.

"You're the house painter, aren't you," she snapped, furrowing her brow. Her eyes widened, seemingly in shock. She took a long drag on her cigarette as it shook in her hand. "I'm sorry, so sorry, I didn't mean to snap like that."

"It's okay," I said. "I just wanted to make sure we were understanding each other."

"Right, of course," she said looking for somewhere to put her dragged out cigarette. I offered her my coffee cup. It was cold anyway.

"You know you shouldn't be smoking in here," I said gently. Hoping not to provoke her, but also not wanting to get kicked out. I rather liked the place. Usually, it was quiet in the middle of the night. But not tonight.

She pursed her lips and bit back some snark, I thought. Instead she opened her bag and took out an envelope. Sliding it across the table.

I took the envelope and looked inside. I tried to play it cool but I probably swallowed a little hard. Inside was a photo of a man in front of a house, an address, and ten grand. I swallowed again. I looked up at her and she seemed nervous at my reaction.

"Is it enough?" She had shut her bag and was holding on tightly, her knuckles white from her grip. "I can get more, but it'll take some time."

"No, this'll cover it," I said and smiled brightly. "One coat or two?"

Stranger in
the Dark

THINGS ARE STRANGER IN the dark. Tried and true, I can vouch for that.

Want to add an extra layer of spooky to anything? Turn out the lights. Want to put people on edge? Stick them in the dark. Want to elicit dread terror? Make the light flicker.

I tapped my little pocket flashlight as the batteries gave out. It rattled when I shook it, but the juice was gone. Our world shrank to the wan cone of light coming from Molly's phone. Handy app, as Molly always has, but their reach just doesn't cut it when you're looking for a way out.

"Are you sure it's this way," I asked Molly. I tended to wander where I wanted with little intent. Precision wasn't my strong suit. She had a specific goal in mind.

"According to the blueprints from 1975, yes." She'd gone through the city archives, familiarizing herself with the flatiron. "It should be right through here." Molly swung her light close to the wall, looking for the door latch. More like a panel than door.

"That was a while ago. Could it have changed?" I didn't want to be trapped in a wall because someone decided to rearrange the building and not file the proper paperwork.

"I was just here the other day," she countered, a bit coolly. Maybe I was imagining things, or maybe I was projecting. The *other day* would have been while I was gone without her. Either way, I left it be. "It was just about..."

Click.

"Got it!" The panel swung open. These old buildings were full of disused access ways, decommissioned utility runs, the occasional fallout shelter. They were second home to Molly, who now used them to sneak her way around pesky things like guards and security and people with clipboards.

We exited the passage into a darkened room supposedly on the sixth floor.

Molly screamed, crashing back into me as she ran from the form looming in the shadows before her. In the dim glow cast by her dropped phone, I saw slavering jaws dripping with blood opened wide, ready to consume. Terrible eyes glinted red.

She thrashed as my heart pounded, tangling her limbs in mine trying to get away. The creature loomed, still. Though it made not a sound.

"Molly," I tried to calm her as she scrabbled backward. "Molly," I drew it out and tapped her leg as she curled in a defensive ball. She kicked me. "Molly! It's not real."

"Ih...wha?" She peeked between her fingers and uncurled a bit.

"It's fake," I said, getting up to inspect the terror that still had not moved. In my experience, things that go bump also give chase. "It's a costume." I picked up the clawed glove hanging from the mannequin. "Rar," I playfully swiped at Molly.

"I thought this was a detective flick." Molly brushed herself off and retrieved her phone. "Damn it, it cracked," she pouted at her broken screen.

I shrugged. Molly wanted to meet one of the actors in the film shooting in the flatiron and got the clever notion to bypass the line of adoring fans using her intimate knowledge of the building.

The door opened, outlining a person in the hallway. A person with a clipboard.

"What are you doing in here? Was that you screaming?"

"Sorry," Molly said, then turned on her charm. "I was just practicing. This guy was great motivation." She grabbed the costume head off the mannequin and hugged it like a favorite plushy. A horrific favored plushy.

"You know you're not supposed to touch the props," the clipboard wielding authority said, taking the head away. "And you're late for wardrobe," she chided. "I found 'em," she said into a headset walkie. "Two more extras coming your way."

I didn't correct her. Molly kept her mouth shut, too, as we followed the production assistant — I think that's what she was. No handy name tag apparent — to wardrobe.

"That was a great scream, by the way." She lightened her tone as we walked. Molly brightened.

"Thanks! I'm hoping to get noticed a little," Molly said, belying her true objective of stealth. Better to blend in once discovered though. Good play.

"Doubt that's going to happen with this B-flick," the P.A. grumbled. "But you never know," she one-eightied. A bit of optimism from a crushed soul. Perhaps she, too, had once hoped to get noticed. "Come on."

She led us through the flatiron, this floor given to impromptu set and film studio. The room we'd come out in turned into prop storage, another makeup, a third was the green room where the object of Molly's quest waited for his closeup. No doubt she'd hope to make her way in there unobstructed but was denied. Likely for the best.

I didn't particularly feel like being arrested for accessory to...whatever Molly did.

This guy was a big deal to her, it seemed. Star of a childhood favorite. He seemed a decent fellow, what I knew of him. Had seen him in a few bit parts on tv shows. Always a pleasant treat. I think this was his first non-animated feature film since a string of horror flicks a decade ago.

I was deposited in another converted office marked 'Wardrobe' in sharpied masking tape while Molly was whisked further down. Apparently the P.A. had other plans for her.

Scant few minutes later I was bustled out the door in a three-piece getup, round glasses, and slicked back hair. But no hat. Didn't everyone wear a hat back then? How disappointing.

"Eggs, eggs, fresh off the plant," a familiar voice came from behind, a little to my left. "Get 'em while they're fresh."

A sharp *Crack.*followed by a sucking splash as an extra extra in a newsie hat took one to the face.

I turned to find a tarted-up cigarette girl with short hair and a feathered headband swaying through the crowd with a box of honest to goodness eggs which she delivered with mad bent, though no one seemed to notice.

Everyone struck by the eggs went about their business as if no runny goo dripped from their nose or stained their suit.

"Felix!" Maya bounced her way over to me, taking short hops in tall heels and her even shorter sequined skirt. The very picture of a 1920s flapper. "What are you doing here?"

"New bit in your act?" I waved my hand up and down at her new attire. I hadn't seen this one before.

"You like?" She twirled. "I thought it a perfect fit for the flick."

"Stunning, dear," I told her. She had good taste in the shapes she took. "What *is* this one about anyway? Molly said it was a gritty detective piece, but we saw some kind of movie monster back in props." I wasn't sure exactly what it was supposed to be. It looked like if a werewolf bit a horned goat and the resulting weregoat had mange in addition to a thirst for blood.

"Oh! Shhh...spoilers." Maya looked around as if anyone could actually hear her besides me. That's the trouble with being a — well not exactly a ghost, let's just say she's trapped — intangible. "So, it is a classic gritty noir, but the main guy, the gumshoe, is actually a werewolf, but not just *any* old werewolf, he's a good werewolf who can track down the guilty by their smell."

"Sounds like fun." I looked at the crew bustling about, getting ready for a scene. One of the director chairs gave the movie title as *Stranger by Night*. "So, any luck," I asked Maya. Being stuck twisted just out of perception as she was, she needed someone to notice her.

Unfortunately, I didn't count.

"No," she deflated. "Not yet. I even smacked the star in the face with my chest. Nothing." She sighed and put on a pouty face.

Hard to imagine that was easily ignored, but then most were oblivious to what went on right around them. Even getting titty smacked in the face.

I later learned there was a stir online about a specific scene in the film. Some people claimed it had a fully nude woman prancing about in the background while the movie's producers and director flat out denied such a thing happened, mostly to keep from getting fined. Helped the marketing sales though. Maya pulled out all the stops sometimes.

"Boo!" Molly popped up in front of me, covered in fake blood. "I got promoted to body number three!" She giggled. "I got to be turned over in the scene," she twirled, showing off the special effects. "He touched me! Oh, I'm never washing this off."

I was glad to see a bit of Molly's sparkle back. She'd been rather displeased at my sudden departure. Not that she said anything about it — or likely would. She'd already had — and won — all the arguments regarding my absence in her head, so she felt no need to repeat herself. Best to just move on with life. Try to pick up where we left off.

"Wish someone would touch *me*," Maya winked from the side, drawing me back to the moment. She made a kissy face and pinched Molly on the backside. Nothing. Not-exactly-ghosts know few boundaries, I've learned. Just the ones that trap them.

Molly sat swooning on the sidelines while I did my bit, staring at the star. Not much. No lines. Just a bunch of hot lights and drinking the same cup of stale coffee over and over. By the time I'd finished take number whatever, someone had apparently convinced her to shower and change — maybe they wanted their prosthetics back?

I finished up and went over to perhaps bask in the afterglow of her glorious performance as body number three. Rebuild some positive association. But the magic of the moment had worn off.

We stood awkwardly in front of the elevator. No history lesson on the operation or installation of this particular model. No ogling the deco detailing of the doors or the floor indicator hands. Silence.

Ding. Finally, our floor, after a drawn-out eternity.

"Hey, it's still here!" On the elevator ride down, I played the piano. It'd been there since I met Maya that foggy night Molly thought I ghosted her. Hadn't felt like moving it after. Glad I didn't.

"Why on earth is there a piano in an elevator?" Molly listened as I tickled the ivories in classic fashion. A small smile turned the corner of her mouth.

We rode up and down and I continued to play as the doors opened and shut on each floor called. A tip in the jar for my troubles.

"What was that all about," she asked as I left with the tip. Molly was used to my, let's say, idiosyncrasies. But it was good to see they had some charm left.

I shrugged. "You once asked how I got out."

Stony Meadows

SPLAT!

"How does this always end up happening?" I wiped goo from my face.

"Incoming!" Molly ducked her head back in the Gator.

I swerved to dodge. The orange missile clipped the roof in its descent, rocking the UTV. We almost tipped but I managed to keep us upright. I gunned it, trying to escape the line of fire.

Orange rinds exploded around us, goo flying everywhere. Molly spat seeds out of her mouth.

"Not that way! Get us closer, Felix," Molly shouted as I jumped the hill, sliding down the backside for some cover from their cannons.

"I'm sneaking around from the other side," I said as the pumpkin barrage quietened. 'Twas a brilliant plan — can't hit what they can't see, right? It would have worked. Stupid trebuchet.

Arcing down from above, the hail of pumpkins pelted our ride.

"Feeeelixx," Molly cried, bracing for the impact.

Bang bang bang. Splats followed suit as the gourds exploded around us.

"Damn idjits threw the whole patch at us!" We were still mobile though, squelching through the guts now marring the field.

"So many wasted pies," Molly shook her head.

"HOOOOOWEEEE!" The talkie squawked. "Got ya!"

A beat-up old farm truck crashed out of the brush; engine roaring as it flung mud from spinning tires. This two-tone Toyota from the seventies or eighties, circa Fall Guy — I'd had the same truck as a kid, only matchbox sized. — gave chase.

Mounted in the back was a turret surrounded by a bunch of air tanks. Mobile punkin chunkin at its finest, devised by a redneck artificer extraordinaire.

Emmett's contraptions had won many a Stony Meadow Pumpkin Brawl over the years. He'd built the spring leaf crossbow the Malloy brothers used with devastating accuracy — three brothers, one to load, one to aim, and one to wind back astride the converted dirt bike motor.

The trebuchet that had just pelted us was a classic design of Emmett's from one of the first Brawls, back when it was just a distance hurled sorta competition. It'd grown to the spectacle I now found myself in when a stray golf cart entered the range by mistake and gave them a moving target. Ever since, the pumpkin artillery had become much more advanced and refined, with a few missteps.

And explosions.

Emmett was the reason propane was banned. There's a sign and everything. It reads:

No propane or other combustible propellants allowed, Emmett."

Emmett had no eyebrows, still.

He had the sort of expressive face that makes brilliant use of bushy eyebrows. Lacking them, his expression reminded me more of a mole as he trained his compressed air punkin chunker on our Gator.

"Surrender?" The talkie squawked again.

I killed the engine. I knew when I was done.

"You got me," I told him.

"What're you doing? We could have made it!" Molly crossed her arms and sulked in the seat beside me. Strands of pumpkin guts clung to her hair.

"Maybe," I said, wiping a seed off her face, "maybe not." By myself, I maybe could have cheated, twisting around unnoticed until I made it to the goal. But that would have been pretty suspicious, and I didn't want Molly slipping through on accident.

"If you'd kept going inside their treb range, we could have." Pouting intensified. "We'd lost him in the woods."

"Shoulda, coulda, woulda," I said. "We'll know better next time."

"We're coming back next year?" This she brightened at. Mostly the money, I think.

If you make it to the goal, you win a cash prize. Have to motivate idiots to play target somehow, don't they?

"Sure, now let's hobble back and enjoy the rest of this festival."

The Brawl itself was the marquee event, but Stony Meadows put on quite the shindig around it.

Pie eating contests, chicken bingo, sack races, you name it.

First stop, obviously, the petting zoo. Molly's mantra.

"Pet all the things!" She raised her fist in the air and dashed ahead.

If it was fluffy, she wanted to pet it. Sometimes when it wasn't. I'd seen her pet snakes and lizards. Not as gleefully though. There must be something about soft fur, especially baby fur.

"Look at the goats! And sheep! And a llama," she giddied. The musky smells of animals wafted my way, as did the tasty ones from the stall next door.

"Putting the barbecue tent next to the petting zoo is a bit on the nose, don't you think?"

Molly didn't pay attention. Instead, she was up to her neck in kebabs in waiting as she waded through the goats to get to the sheep. One of them head butted a kid — of the human variety — who started wailing.

"That one's traumatized," I muttered.

My own charge turned and cuffed the bully goat and hoisted the kid up. "No," she told the startled goat. The goat went myaaahh in protest. "You're okay sweetie," she told the little boy, taking him to the edge of the pen.

"You don't take no shit from goats, do you?" Gentle, animal-loving Molly hadn't held back either.

"You literally can't, they'll do whatever they want if you let them," she said. "Besides, the goat is totally fine, they have super hard heads." Molly scratched the bully goat's chin after the human kid had run away. "Now play nice," she admonished it.

"I'm going for some goat on a stick, or in sandwich form," I pointed at the source of the tasty smells. "Want something?"

"Myaaa'aaah," she shook her head no, already conversing with the goats. I wandered while she debated whatever astute observations the goats made about various grass and shrubberies. Because I guess that's what goats talk about?

The guy behind the counter, his name was Steve according to yet another name tag, wore a t-shirt that read 'I'd smoke that' accompanying a diagram of a cow illustrating the various cuts. I felt confident he knew what he was doing — unlike myself when I ran Mallorey's — so when he handed me a sandwich and explained it contained pulled goat slow cooked in root beer, I took a large bite without hesitation.

Fireworks. Mind blowing flavor. Sweet and so, so tender. Steve knew his meat — a sentiment I tried to convey to him, though it came out rather garbled around mouthfuls of delicious goat. He seemed used to this and accepted the praise while spreading the gospel of smoked goat to others of the masses.

I licked my fingers clean one at a time and wiped away the drool dripping from the corners of my mouth as I wandered the festival. I came upon the rabbit races next.

I watched a couple of heats, made some bets. I liked one named Ernie, he seemed to have spunk, but Terry crushed them all in the finals. The one wearing a bib marked 99 came in last — likely destined for Steve's pot.

The day wore away. Molly caught up to me as I said hello to Biscuit and Gravy — two chickens clucking away by a lady selling eggs. I did a double take to make sure she wasn't Maya, ready to chuck them. No, she was legit one hundred percent grade A farmer. She did not wear a helpful name tag but thought her name was Rachel or something with an R anyway. Much better when people wore name tags.

"Let's do the maze!" Molly clamped onto my arm. "It'll be fun," she promised.

"I don't know about that." I had my doubts. Mazes could be dangerous places. Getting all turned about. The hurdygurdyist confirmed my suspicions.

"Blood a'the Wisps do flicker an' flick

Tils they twist your light away.

T'the other side of what, who knows,

You see, you see, you seeee"

Not creepy in the slightest. No. Harmless little tales. A few refrains passed as we walked closer to the maze entrance.

"I am the righteous hand, forgot,

And the only path you've got.

Don't you turn your back on me,

You see, you see, you'll see."

Folk songs and cryptic warnings. Hand in hand. Molly took mine to drag me further along.

The corn was dead, as is often the case in these things. Brown and dried. Ears long gone. Tassels tossed aside in the rubbish or for the pigs. Do pigs eat corn tassels? They eat pretty much everything else.

Focus. I had let my mind wander. Molly was talking but I found it supremely hard to focus on what she said. Not that I didn't want to, but things were getting a little fuzzy.

The path cut through the dead tall grass — corn is a grass you know? Not sure if it's high as an elephant's eye, but it was tall none-the-less. I said that already. About it being tall. Something wasn't right. I felt pulled at my edges.

I stumbled.

Red flashed by, bumping me to the side.

I fell to one knee, looking up in time to see the hind end of an animal draped in cloth.

Molly ran after the blur. "Oh, the poor dear is caught." The words trailed after her. "Felix, we have to help it." Almost an echo.

From the right? Or had she left the path to cut through the stalks?

"Molly?" I called out. "Which way'd you go?"

"Over here!" Her reply came from both left and right. Shit.

"Where's here?" I tried to level my tilted head, suppressing the dread as it built. That wasn't right. Rustles to my left.

"Boo!" Molly jumped from the dead stalks, laughing as she tried to tickle me.

"What're you doing?" I fended off her fingers seeking soft spots.

"Oh lighten up," she rolled her eyes. "Jump scares are Halloween 101."

"It's not Halloween yet," I said. Samhain had a particular meaning tugging at my brain. I couldn't quite grasp it.

"September counts," Molly said. "We annexed it when Christmas set up a beachhead in July." She was apparently a fan. "The battle for August has begun."

"Bit dramatic," I observed.

"Christmas is supposed to be special," she huffed. "What's the point if it's year round? It'd lose meaning. But Halloween is a total mood." Molly nodded with finality.

"You do decorate with ravens," I said. She did have several of the birds wired to various heights in her abode. I'd thought it had come about after her journey through the cryptid rabbit hole, but apparently it ran much deeper.

"Yes." Was all she said on the matter. "Come on, I need your help," she said, taking me truly inside of the maze.

"Help with what?" The world shrank, not two feet in front of me. Dried corn stalks smacked my face as we broke through to the distressed animal. I heard commotion carry through the rustling of our passage.

"It's caught, all tangled up and crying." Faintly I heard the mewling. Followed by some yips that did not come from whatever had brushed by me. More yips and a squeak as we pushed into a circle in the corn.

Molly froze. Dread filled her eyes.

What looked like a fox stood at the edge. Another behind, concealed, and two to the left. A crow cawed overhead, not scared of the people now in the field.

"Not a fox," she whispered, confirming my fear. She clutched for my hand, her nails digging in. She'd seen its like before.

In the middle turned round and round an antlered or horned something, caught. Its hind hooves churned the ground to mud. The not-a-fox stepped forward, eyes beginning to glow. Too many eyes.

I looked for a way out, but no part of the maze led to this circle. It was not on the path. No way forward, our only choice back.

"We have to go," I said, tugging Molly back into the concealing field.

The baby animal bawled, wrapped in red, terror laced through the cry as if it sensed the not-a-fox draw near.

"We can't leave it." Molly's eyes implored me. "They'll kill it."

"You don't know what those things are," I told her. I did, and it was not good. Our best bet was to vamoose while they were distracted by the helpless prey.

I did something stupid. Really stupid. Kids, don't try this at home.

I went for my belt, the snapping threat that shut every kid of my generation up. Flicking the buckle loose, I tugged it free of the loops with a whoosh of leather on denim.

Stepping into the circle, I snapped my belt at the not-a-fox — I really need a better name for them — leather cracking the air. Its lip curled back, black spotted with red, baring fangs of glinting metal. It hissed.

It hissed like ripping paper, spittle spraying the air. The straw on which it landed sizzled and smoked, acrid curls rising.

SNAP again, another step forward, keeping the belt taut 'tween me and them. Snap snap.

One lunged from the side, quieter than the rest — cunning — going for my leg. Back I kicked, boot catching it between the too many eyes. It yowled in pain, scattering brush as it landed, scrabbling to be away.

Snap snap. Whip-crack.

I moved closer to the mewling sounds, step by step, not taking my eyes from the threat from circle's edge.

"Felix!" Molly's own cry, a rising crescendo, saved my stupid ass.

The red cloth flapped back, fangs and claws bared to attack, no longer concealed beneath.

"How pretty the sound the squish you make will be," the Bloodybell said, flexing its claws. Part goat — its horns swept back — part goblin, sadistic and evil. The creature mewled like a babe yet again before croaking a laugh at its own cruel joke.

It leapt. Fingers like knives reached for my throat, I barely dodged with a roll to my side.

"Leave me be!" I yelled, springing up. Faint memory taking hold.

"What the ever-loving fuck is that?"

"Why Bill o'deSoul, be I," it hissed. Teeth like torn bone, grating. "And who be ye?"

"DON'T!" I snapped my buckle at its head. "Don't answer," I told Molly. Fur flashed in again from the side. Stomping boots stomped. I couldn't keep this up.

"Leave me be." I said it again, dancing back toward Molly.

"Oh kindness, ye sir," this creature began. It sharpened its claws, a skiss and shnak. "Do spare a pence, perhaps," it said in old form. The ritual coming to mind. There were rules to which it was bound.

"A coin," I said to Molly. "It wants a coin." It would straight up murder us if we didn't abide the forgotten customs. Memories tugged at me, loosening. It was counting on our ignorance, I knew.

"I don't have any coins!" She patted her non-existent pockets in vain. "I don't do physical."

"Small kindness if ye please." This Bill o'deSoul stepped forward, persistent. Claws stretched out, palm up. His bloody red cape draped down his shoulders.

Coin. Coin. Where was a coin?

Without thinking, I acted, stepping toward the razor sharp claws and grinding bone teeth. Up, I reached. Past the top of his head — closer to the stench he breathed out, rot and decay — to curl my fingers over his horns and behind his twitching ear. With a flick of my wrist, I gripped from there cold silver.

This coin, I withdrew, shining and new, to place in his palm.

"A kindness for thee, now leave us be," I spoke to him a third time.

He screwed up his eyes and stared close to mine. His nostrils flared, steaming the air taken chill. Biting the palm-crossed silver.

"Aye, a kindness indeed," he turned on his heel. "And thee shall be remembered."

The Bloodybell sang a familiar tune as it entered the stalks, fading from sight. Yips and yelps rang in from the side, as pair by pair, the glow of the too many eyes vanished.

"You'll see."

Keres Station

GREEN HAIRED GOTH MAYA finished up and swallowed. We had an agreement — I kept her company and she kept me distracted. It wasn't the healthiest relationship, but it worked. Better than getting lost in drink. My opinion.

I always run away. At least with Maya, it's not far. Plus she likes to spice things up in interesting ways which shall be left entirely to your imagination — though I assure you, whatever you picture comes up far short.

Running from problems. That's where I was. Molly had shut herself away after the maze encounter.

"Are we going to talk about that?" She'd asked me that night, her eyes still filled with terror. They darted about, waiting for something else to appear.

"Probably not," I'd said. "No use in dwelling on a murder hobo wanting some drug money." I dissembled. I was good at that. At denying proper and true memory in favor of a convivial lie.

"Right," she'd reluctantly said. Disbelief had begun to take hold as memory rewrote. People, as a general rule, don't do well with the weird. Even Molly, for as much as she'd seen, would chalk that up to a dream. Who has horns?

"I can, if you like, sir," Maya said playfully, looking up at me from my lap.

"That's ok," I patted her hornless head, smoothing the green hair with my hand. She settled again as I ran my fingers over the shaved sides, relishing in the touch of someone who saw her. "Just thinking out loud." I hadn't known I was.

Molly.

One day became two. Now a third had passed. Nothing.

No calls, no texts. Mine unreturned, left on read.

Even the videos I'd sent by way of apology featuring fluffy and fuzzy baby animals remained unwatched. This bothered me.

"Gods fucking... we know!" The room rattled and Maya poofed to the edge of the bed. Her bagpipes in hand, she wailed in retribution. "Fwaaaaaah! Fwaaaaaahh! We know!"

I eyed her. My brow raised. I hadn't heard anything.

"Sorry. It's been driving me crazy the last couple of days." The pipes vanished again. I was about to ask what when I heard it.

A sound — something of a cross between a goose being strangled and a rock crusher. If you could drown a Mac truck, this is the noise it would make, and it was not a good noise to be hearing.

Especially as this one seemed to be quite agitated.

"Are there tunnels here?" It lived in tunnels, I knew. Fog cleared in my brain and something giant that dwelled in tunnels came to mind. Rokuichi, I think it's called. Like those long-bodied Asian dragons, but furry. Wicked beak and flat, dead eyes, you did not want to see one of those coming down the tunnel. Forget the freight train coming your way, this was worse.

"Old access ones?" Maya said with a shrug. "Maybe an old station? I don't know. I just know it's loud and obnoxious and it gives fuckall about who it disturbs — which is mostly me."

I suppose she could hear it much clearer than I could. It was a twisted creature as well, barely perceived by normies — if at all. They'd likely chalk it up to a train rumbling through or a small earthquake if it got really rowdy.

"Hopefully it calms down soon," I said.

"Then maybe I could get some sleep." Maya reappeared in a pink frilly nightgown and curlers, climbing into bed. She also had one of those eye-masks ready to pull down.

"Want me to tuck you in?" I joked. Maya shooed.

"Off with you, I need my beauty rest." She pulled the novelty mask down. It had shut eyes painted on it. Quickly dozing.

We had sex, but there was no attachment to it. Clingy as Maya could be, the novelty of having someone see her seemed to have worn off a bit — especially since I couldn't get her out. Someone who *could* watch her walk around naked might have become a bit invasive to her after years of the utter privacy being unperceived provided. Now we'd fallen into a comfortable rhythm.

Nothing serious.

Puddles lined the street outside the flatiron. It'd rained while Maya and I had been fulfilling our arrangement, reminding me of the night we'd met. At least there wasn't a fog to get twisted up in this time.

I still couldn't believe I'd let that happen. Rookie mistake. I wasn't a rookie but I didn't know it, not at the time. Still don't really. The fog lingers in my head now, not on the street.

At least I'd remembered how to get out without relying on a piano every time. That had come in handy.

I splashed in a puddle. Misstep. It had been raining a lot the last couple of days. Not constant. Hit-or-miss. As soon as one puddle had dried, another took its place. Have to watch out. Never in the same spot twice. That was the funny thing about puddles. No matter the local topography, the puddles were always different, if only slightly.

The city lights danced in the reflection of the ripples, distorting the buildings to some other scene.

I looked away, breaking contact. You just don't go around staring into puddles — who knows where you'll end up.

"Wait a...ah fuck!" Goddamn horseshit fuckity fuck fuck.

And did I mention fuck?

Molly was in trouble. I'd just seen her, a flash of her at least.

No wonder she hadn't watched any of the kitten videos, she couldn't. She'd been below ground from the looks of things. Concrete and darkness. Slipped below. Twisted. And I hadn't noticed.

The ground rumbled.

Pieces fell into place.

I did mention fuck, right? Because fuck.

That woman. She really was the meme.

Pspspspsps.

To a Rokuichi. If it had found her...

I pushed the absolute worst case scenarios from my mind as they sprang up, leaving only the majorly not good scenarios in there to grow.

The fact that it was still rumbling about, warbling like a drowned semi, was now classified as a good thing. Molly would always go toward the sounds of an animal in distress.

If she'd actually found it, the furry giant would be irresistible to pet.

I needed to find her, but where had she slipped through?

"Fuck it." I dove in head first. Leave it up to chance.

Into a puddle and out through its twin with a twist. Not the best way to travel — you end up rather damp, and there's no in-flight drink service. Plus the whole indeterminate destination thing.

I was, indeed, underground. A tunnel of some sort — I'd been right about that. The rumble was louder down here, causing the string fixtures to sway, casting shadows that danced. Hopefully nothing fell.

"I don't like small places," I muttered, looking at the arched stone ceiling I could reach out and touch.

It sounded again. What was a faint cry above pierced my very heart in the reverberating confines I now found myself in. Maya's bagpipes had nothing on an irate Rokuichi. Guarantee I did not want to see the live show.

But I had front row seats. Lucky me.

Dingy white fur covered the sinuous body as it coiled along the tunnel's arch, four seemingly undersized, hairless legs propelling it along, gripping the stone walls. It polished the surface as it moved. I guess there were benefits to letting a giant pipe cleaner live under your city — saved on janitorial.

It turned its massive head to regard me standing in plain view. There were few places to hide in a tunnel like this — it was going to see me regardless, better to let it see me well in advance than startle it. Startling was bad. It was either going to eat my face or pass me by unharmed. Just had to hope long-boy here wasn't hungry.

Pardon me. Long-mama. As she drew closer, I saw the telltale lumps of fur sticking out at odd intervals. She'd just kindled and her young clung to her.

Closer still, the swaying lights glinted off her wicked beak which was now poised to strike. Will she, won't she?

The suspense was killing me.

Her beak cracked wide, maw gaping as she chuffed in my face. Her mane quivered as the sound like a jack-hammer assaulted me, stilling my heart from the sheer pressure of it. Rust filled my nostrils.

I gritted my teeth and stood my ground.

She relented and tasted the air with her tongue, twisting this way and that, coming up beside me. Her flat dead eye took me in from extremely close range. So close I could see my face — still uneaten — reflected in the black depths.

Not finding that which she sought, she moved on. Her fluffy soft fur brushed against me as she passed. I might have found it delightful had I not feared the aforementioned face-eating.

Finally, I exhaled. I'd held my breath the entire time and felt vaguely lightheaded.

My oxygen starved brain recalculated the possible course of events, coming to only one conclusion: Molly had one of the kits.

How she'd come upon it, I had no idea. But long-mama was looking for her baby and was quite agitated about it. She'd apparently been so the last couple of days — the same length as Molly's recent reticence.

And those kits were irresistibly soft. She would absolutely give them all the pets. I needed to find her before long-mama.

"Molly!" No time like the present. "Molly Molly Molly!" Not the time for subtle stealth either. No one was going to hear me down here.

Just Molly and the long fluffy face eater who'd so far been disinterested in me.

I walked for hours, keeping to the smaller tunnels, hoping Molly had as well.

"And I never saw Molly again," I said, "that's how this story is going to go." I was tired of keeping up the running string of commentary in hopes of drawing Molly out. I was beginning to light into a cheese is cheese diatribe in hopes of really riling her up when I faintly heard laughter in the distance.

"Tony stop," Molly laughed, elongating the 'stop' into more of a 'staaaahp,' "that tickles." Followed by more giggles. Ok, she was apparently fine. No need to have worried.

"Molly?" I called into the echoing dark.

"Felix?" A faint reply. "Felix! Is that you?" Louder this time.

"I think it's me, never really sure," I said. "Where are you? Who's Tony?"

"I'm in the catchment basin," she called back. "Tony is...well...I don't know, so I call him Tony." Molly'd definitely stolen the kit. All the pets. I sighed.

"Where?" I had no clue what a 'catchment basin' was. She's the one with the thing for architecture. I probably shouldn't even ask.

"Big hole I'm literally stuck in," she called back. "Don't fall in."

Well why didn't you just say you were stuck in a big hole? I also didn't ask. Instead I walked carefully forward so as *not* to fall in the same hole myself. It didn't sound pleasant.

"How'd you get stuck in a hole?" I asked as I sought, yelling through the echoes.

"I fell *through* a puddle, first of all. Need to ask you about that," she started off. "Then, I heard Tony crying and came down to help," she said. "He was frozen, poor thing. Weren't you." She made some cooing baby noises and a garbage disposal responded. One that had a fork stuck in it. Adorable. "So anyway one thing led to another, the ladder sucks, and I twisted my ankle."

Fell through a puddle. She'd definitely have some questions about that. Plus, I had the feeling she'd glossed over some important bits.

"And I can't get signal down here," she said. I'm surprised she didn't lead with that. Though she wouldn't have gotten signal above ground either. Not twisted as she was.

"Twisted while twisted. Wonderful. Great." I tripped over some junk, sending it flying. Molly cursed.

"Damn it, Felix, be careful." Agitated garbage disposal sounds approached ultrasonic. A rumble in the distance. "You almost hit Tony." She definitely had the lost kit long-mama was looking for. Super.

"Hey, I found you!" I chose to focus on the positive of having found her instead of the impending furry freight train that may soon bear down upon us. "Progress!" I moved along the trajectory the junk had taken from my toe to Molly.

She was indeed in a hole. One a dozen feet deep. She sat upon a suitcase above the waterline while Tony munched on a lunch cooler. Slender and white, maybe as long as my arm. Less grungy than his mama. His beak worked to dissect the plastic into smaller bits which he nommed on — thankfully — instead of Molly's face.

"Dining in?" I motioned to the chip bag and half eaten sandwich on the wrapper next to Tony with his snack. The baby Rokuichi writhed as he ripped into his meal. They'll eat anything.

"Tony's such a good boy," she pet him. "Aren't you, aren't you." She scooped him up and into her hoodie for snuggles.

Happy disposal noises followed. Called it. "He's been bringing me food," she said.

Of course Molly would wind up with a Rokuichi nursemaid. She's Molly. I moved past that. I'd ask her for details later, but from what I could see, the bits of ladder left were missing a few of the rungs that should be sticking out of the wall like staples. I doubt she could have made it back up even without a twisted ankle.

I lay on the concrete, peering down into the basin which apparently caught stuff in storm runoff — hence the name. Natural feeding grounds for Tony and his kin. Long-mama had probably left all the kits to munch and he hadn't come when called.

"So how do we get you out? I can't exactly climb down and get you."

"There should be a hook for a cleaning chain," she thought for a minute. "But they usually take those with them. I dunno, any magic scarves up your sleeve?"

"Fresh out." I waved my hands to show they were empty. Would that I could conjure a rope of some sorts. There weren't any chains lying about. Or ropes. I hadn't seen anything resembling one since... "Be right back." I had an idea.

A bright one.

Upon my return, I tossed the strand of work lights I'd pillaged over the edge of the hole. Molly grabbed the cord, wrapping it around her waist and under her butt. I began hauling her up.

"Thanks for the lift," she said, mounting the edge.

"I am now keeper of the bright ideas," I said "Thank you very much."

I held out my hand to help her up. Tony snipped at it from her hoodie pouch.

"Tony!" Molly snapped at the kit like it was just an errant puppy. To my surprise, it listened. Tony relented and I helped Molly to her feet, lending her an arm for support.

"You know you can't keep him," I said before she could ask. The tunnel rumbled again. More rock crusher than goose this time. "His mama's been looking for him." I looked pointedly at the walls, only partly because I wanted to make sure they weren't crumbling. "And you don't want to mess with mama."

"Mothers always like me," Molly sniffed and turned up her nose.

"One day you may not be so lucky," I said.

"Guess I should stick close to you." She smiled and looked my way. Dimples formed in her cheeks.

Tony picked then to leap out of Molly's pouch and scamper away. Guess he doesn't like the mushy bits.

"Tony!" Molly started to go after him, but I held her hand.

He looked back, then ducked through a side pipe and the rock crusher squealed, shaking the whole ground, happy to have her baby home again.

"He needed to get home for dinner," I said. Molly sighed for a moment.

"While we're down here," Molly began, hobbling beside me. "I heard there's like this abandoned train station we should totally check out. Keres Station, I think..."

Lenore's

MY CONSCIOUSNESS FLED AS Elliot kept watch from his post by the door. I sat, given to nod. Briefly my mind flitted amongst entertaining and charming dreams, a few salacious, but mostly ran parallel to the course of reality, drifting only slightly as I skimmed.

Lenore's was the only place I felt safe to do this, confident my little corner of reality would remain inviolate as I dozed in the warm sun beaming through the book stacks occluding the window. Elliot leapt from the floor to my lap, rubbing against my hand for a scratch. Apparently it was time to wake.

"There you are!" Molly leaned around the corner, her eyes only for Elliot, I just happened to be present as well. Barely rating an acknowledgement, myself, she scooped the tabby from my lap and coddled it. I stretched in the sunshine, careful not to disturb the finely arranged piles surrounding me. I'd been researching the gentleman I'd encountered in Vegas and the recipe he'd left for me at the strip club. Books on alchemy were quite scarce, it seemed, though it was apparently quite in vogue

"Hello to you, too," I said, gathering the fine cup and saucer that had until recently held equally fine tea. There are few places I feel utterly rooted to this world, and this is one.

Lenore's Used Books. It's a real bookshop. There's only one left, wherever you're at. You should all go. You know the one I'm talking about.

It's a quiet place tucked away in several rooms spread among two and a half, or three floors of the honest to goodness shopping arcade, the same circa as the flatiron. A matched pair, almost, of a time I wish would come again. Labyrinthine stacks lead to cozy nooks and hidden rooms among the ever shifting piles. You'll always find the book you need at Lenore's because, let's be honest, it will find you.

Marty is immortal, I feel sure. As untouched by time as the classics lining these shelves. He's told numerous customers numerous times about his prophesied death.

"Oh yeah, I know how it happens," Marty said to yet another customer. It's one of his old chestnuts. "Once I get each book priced and properly sorted on the shelf —" he made a croaking sound and snapped his eyes shut "— that's it. Just keel over and done." I heard him talking down the hall as he introduced a new denizen to the maze.

I surreptitiously pull a few books from the shelf every time he tells the story. Not that I really have anything to worry about, I've seen the stacks and stacks and more stacks of boxes of used books that never grows smaller in the back rooms. Always more to feed the shelves, including my own.

"Ah, Felix," Marty said, seeing me with my empty cup of tea. "This is Felix, one of the local authors on the shelf I showed you earlier," he told the book browser. "Take your time, look around, you'll happen on your book by chance. People always do."

"You know that's what gave me the title idea, right?" It just worked perfectly, to be honest. I've heard Marty say it so many times, it just stuck.

"I read the latest dedication, Felix. That's about as far as I got." Very matter of fact, was Marty, straight to the heart. "Sorry," Marty looked at me apologetically. "Nothing against it, and I'll get through it, just..."

I forestalled him, knowing where he was going. I'd seen people pick it up and put it right back down. Like most of my words. Disinterest plain on their face.

"Marty, I'm not hurt by the ones who don't like it." It had taken a bit to get there, but it was true. "I write them for the people for whom it becomes their favorite. For those who cling to that book like a lifeline. There are plenty of people out there no one is writing for. I write for them."

I also write for myself. I can't not. I spent too long suppressing it, feeling unequal to the task, but then it all slipped away. One day you just wake up and realize there's no more time to do the things you want to do. So quit making excuses and do them!

"Well I think it's great, Felix," Molly said. "Ten out of ten, would recommend." She swung the tabby around like a dance partner through the aisles. Elliot didn't seem to mind. "But I can't believe you told them I slept through meeting Bigfoot. That never happened," she chided me.

"I didn't," I feigned innocence. I changed all the names to protect the people involved. Any resemblance to actual events or persons, alive or dead, yadda-yadda is purely coincidental. I never spill tea.

The last time I told anyone the actual details about anything, the historic line of spider guardians came to a tragic end. Never again.

I'd written a little blog post when I first started toying with putting words in particular orders about a spider in the men's room at work. It lived in this little groove the grout made between the tiles, a sort which led under the edge of the heater under the window. I'd seen it poke its head and front legs out from the warmth, waiting for gnats and the like. Year after year, it was there every winter when the heater warmed the hole. Or at least a spider stalked the grout lines in the men's room at my work.

This was the crux of the post — me postulating whether this was indeed the same spider, ancient for its kind, or rather a generational legacy of spiders, guardianship passed down the family line. Fun little thought experiment and literary tangent to traverse, but it ended in travesty.

After posting the piece, the spider vanished. Never to be seen again. I feared it my fault, having drawn too much attention to its no-longer-eternal-vigil. Brought death down upon my friend(s) — I never learned whether it was the one or many spiders.

And so I lie. I lie for your protection. It's best you not know how the trick is done because the unwary tend to have their face eaten by what goes bump in the night. Burp.

Molly harrumphed. I'd lied to her long enough. It had been detrimental to her of late and a reckoning was due. Time to get to the business at hand.

These shelves contained words which unlocked something within me. Sharpened my saw. Primed that word well for drawing forth fresh thought. A feeling that would have to wait. Though they were made of wood, the books herein were remarkably unhylic. There's that word again.

Hylics are empty, devoid of soul. By the very act of their creation, books are not. Imbued with the spark of their creator. Some people have one book inside them. Others have several. Cigar chomping monkeys have a fraction of one to imbue the typed page. People like myself — and apparently Molly — burgeon with that ineffable spark that becomes smothered in so many.

It had gotten Molly in over her head. And it had been my fault.

"Time to get lost," I gently took Elliot from her arms. "Lead on my friend."

The tabby cat scooted from sight. I eyed Molly and waved my hand in an 'after you.'

"What?"

"He's twisting away." Her eyes widened. She bolted after the cat.

"Elliot!" She knocked a stack over in pursuit. "Waaaaaiiiittt."

The stacks were calling me, their worlds awaiting but a breadth of sunlight on the pages. I wouldn't mind a little Van Winkle time among them, but Molly might be perturbed. She hated missing out on things.

I shrugged as Martin looked at the fallen pile of books spilling into the aisle. "What can I say, we love you and want to keep you around a little longer," I said by way of explanation as I turned and walked away backwards, not helping to rehabilitate the scattered tomes, and went after Molly.

Elliot scampered his way through the maze as only a cat knows how. Poking his head back around bends just to see if Molly followed. Almost taunting her.

"Here pspspsps," she called when she lost sight. "Come here pretty boy...pspspsps."

"He's not a mountain lion, Molly," I said in reference. "Though that's totally how you're going to go." I thumbed through a book on wildebeest on the Serengeti from the seventies as she looked for the wayward tabby.

"I mean," she didn't even deny it. "Pet all the things. That's my motto."

"All the things," I nodded. That had gotten her in trouble more than once.

"Aha!" Molly spotted a tiny gap between a shelf and the wall that was filled with books except for a small opening at the bottom. "Are you hiding in here little man?" She excavated more books from the gap and crawled in on her hands and knees, her phone light shining ahead, shimmying her way through.

I took a little short cut, twisting to the other side, and offered her a hand up as she emerged.

"Thanks," she said, thinking nothing of it for several seconds before it hit. "Wait just a damn second." She looked down at the hole from which she'd emerged. Not nearly big enough for me to fit. "How..."

"Magic," I waved jazz hands at her. "Now, feel that fuzz behind your ear?"

She reached up, stroking her hair.

"No. Inside." I tapped my head. "It's like the hum of an electric fence."

Molly looked puzzled. "Purple sparks?" She squinted and twinged.

"Bzzap," I said. "Can be. Touch synesthetic," I said. "An amalgam of senses rewired to cope with something a mite incomprehensible."

"Looks pretty comprehensible to me," Molly said. She looked around this hidden room full of even more books. I doubted any customers had been here for quite a while. Maybe not even Marty. Might've been Lenore's special place.

"Look again," I pointed behind her. She twisted her head about and the room went red. A window appeared in the wall of books behind Molly.

"Where did that come from?" She peered through the window to see the animatronic shells of people parading about. Bustling on the city street. Eating at cafe tables on sidewalks. One or two occasionally shone blue as the scenes shifted like slides.

"The question is where did you come from so that you now see it." She'd had tastes of other before. Unintentional. Glimpsed only in passing.

"I don't understand."

"I don't expect you to understand," I said. "Even I don't understand. But I know." Cryptic much?

"How can you know something you don't understand?" Puzzlement screwed her face.

"Now that's the trick," I said, leading to the door now to my left. She followed. "It's feeling more than thought. Bit of detachment. A bit unhinged," I swung the door open. White light bathed us. "You just do," I said, stepping back into the bookstore, "and you're done."

I didn't know it all myself. Those memories were muffled. Locked away. Whatever I'd learned at Saffron's was lost to my waking self. My higher functions. Ingrained instead in synapse and bone. Bits and pieces of things bubbled free, more of late as the world seemed to wake. More as I'd encountered and just knew what to do. My meeting with the Count had jarred more than a few things loose, confronted with the irrefutable as I'd been.

"But how?" Molly still tried to rationalize. This was going to be a tough lesson.

"I can't make you learn and I can't do it for you, not anymore," I said. "You're just going to have to figure it out. You've a knack for this sort of thing, and I would know."

I led Molly to the front shelves of Lenore's where a customer perused my book.

"Oooh look Felix," Molly said giddily. He set it down again and she pounced. "You know," she began her pitch. "It's a charming little book really. Relaxed, but tickles the fancies. In fact, I could get the author to sign a copy to y..." She trailed off as the guy turned and walked away. "Rude."

I waited for realization. Behind schedule.

"He just turned and walked away. Didn't even say a word!" Molly huffed, hands on her hip. "Can you believe that?"

This last she directed at Marty. He was gently flipping pages in a book to be priced. Carefully running his fingers down the text, lovingly smoothing the edge down before turning the next. A bit of a water stain — perhaps from tears at a poignant moment — he noticed. But Molly, he noticed not.

"Your first lesson," I said to my student. "How to get out."

Lessons to Learn

I THINK I BROKE her brain.

"Get out of where?" She turned round and looked, expecting boogeymen and seeing only bookstore.

"Here," I tapped Marty on the shoulder. He didn't respond. *Ting-a-ling.* A customer came in. I punched him in the face. He didn't respond. "Wherever here is," I said.

I hadn't recalled it immediately myself when I slipped through the fog months back. A bit more filled the gaps, puzzle pieces falling into place to form more than that kitten. I still don't know what it's called, just that it's *here*.

I stepped out from behind a shelf.

"Ack!" Marty jumped. Molly jumped, too. "Felix, don't scare an old man like that."

"Sorry, Marty," I said, taking a book from the shelf. "There, now you'll be fine." I placed it on the floor. "Have you seen Molly?"

"Felix, I'm right here," Molly said.

"No, not since she went chasing Elliot," Marty laughed. "That girl and her animals. Reminds me a bit of her. Lenore loved her aminals," he said. "She always switched the m and n to be cute," he added by way of explanation.

"I'd like to have known her," I said. I would have. Anyone who amassed this caliber of library was okay by me.

"Hellooooo," Molly waved, not listening. "I'm right here." Elliot sauntered in and stared straight at Molly. "Thank you, Elliot," Molly said. He mrowed. "See, he can see me," she said to Marty.

"She'd have liked you I think," Marty said. "Had a soft spot for...well." He waved at me up and down. I didn't quite know how to take that.

"Well," I said, letting it slide. "If you see Molly," I said, scratching Elliot behind the ears, "let her know I had to get going."

"Will do," Marty laughed. "Girl's probably lost in another book." I laughed. Molly didn't.

"Something like that," I said and waved as I *ting-a-linged* myself out. Pausing just long enough for Molly to slip out behind me.

"Okay, what gives," she said, rounding on me.

"You slipped through, again," I said. "At least this time you were marginally aware of it. Purple sparks," I reminded her. "Pay attention to those."

"So...I'm a ghost?" She waved her hand in front of a guy hurrying on the street and almost got clipped by a bike in the process. "Jackass!" She yelled at the guy who didn't hear.

"Not a ghost," I said. That seemed to be everyone's first reaction, even mine. "Did you die?"

"I don't think so," she patted her discorporated self. "Unless a pile of books fell on me? Do you remember it when you die?" She was quick to tangent.

"Can't say as I'd know, not having died to my knowledge." I may have forgotten a lot, but I'm reasonably certain I haven't died. By strange chance. "No, you're just caught in between. Different by one twisted molecule is how I rationalize it."

"Hence 'twisted'?" She was picking up the bits I'd let slip and piecing them together. Molly was an excellent puzzler.

"Just out of perception," I amended. "You can interact a bit, but for some reason people's minds slide right off you."

"Elliot saw me," Molly said.

"Cats see everything," I said. They did. It's not exactly ghosts they're staring at like that. Though sometimes... "Animals, in general, are an exception."

"Cool!" Molly clapped with a bit of glee. "What else can I do?" She pressed against a brick wall, trying to walk through. "Can't pass through walls."

"Careful dear," I led her away from the brick wall. "There's lots of things you can do, and most will get you in trouble. This is not somewhere you want to get *lost* or *stuck*."

"But no one can see me?"

"Typically, no. That's the trick you need to learn though. How to get out."

"So how do I get out?"

"There is no method, you just get out."

"Great, what's the trick?"

"That would be a method and there is no method," I said, upping the crypticism in my voice. "You need someone to notice you."

"You notice me," Molly said. "Can I get out now?"

"I don't count," I said. "You need someone unaware."

"How can they notice me if they're unaware?" Molly began to huff at the illogic loop.

"That's the trick," I said sagaciously.

Hours passed. Molly tried many things to gain attention, catch someone's eye. I bit my tongue at her antics. My favorite was when she zip tied three grocery carts to some a-hole who'd parked across two spaces — one of them handicapped. *I've always wanted to do that.* Molly had said. I couldn't contain myself. People must have thought I was a loon, laughing at thin air.

Her, they did not notice.

"This sucks!" Molly flopped on the bench beside me. "How can they see you and not me?"

"I got out hours ago." Startling Marty had done the trick for me. Subtlety was the key. Not that I was going to tip my hand to Molly. Not yet. She needed to learn for when I wasn't around.

"How?"

"Mysterious ways," I nodded and waved the question off. "No cheating."

"Tellll meeee," she whined.

I smiled, also cryptically.

"Fine, keep your secrets," she memed. "I rather like people not bothering me and being able to enact my vengeance upon bad parkers. I still have my animals." She cooed at a pigeon she'd lured with bread. "Plus, it'll make sneaking into buildings *soooo* much easier," she brightened.

"That it would," I said. "But there are some drawbacks." I handed her the book I was reading. One of the sole alchemical texts I'd been able to find at Lenore's, more of a primer than anything particular. She thumbed through the pages and scowled.

"It's all gibberish," she said, checking the cover to see what book I'd handed her. "Foreign language?"

"You know how when you try to read in a dream, the words all slide away and get squiggly," I said. "Yeah, that."

Apparently, she hadn't noticed she couldn't read anything all day long, focused on the task as she was. I can't blame her, who notices you can't read in a dream until you actually try to read in the dream?

"But wait, there's more," I said. "Check your phone. It hasn't dinged at you all day."

"It's on silent, duh," she said, pulling out her phone. "Who lets their phone..." she trailed off. "No signal." She tapped at the screen. Nothing. Panic filled her eyes at her lacking apps.

"Not so appealing now, is it?" I rather liked it myself, but I wasn't addicted to my phone quite like some others I know. But there were other risks. "Come on," I said. "I want you to meet someone."

Maya was singing cabaret on the empty bar when we got up to the top of the flatiron. All boots and tassels and the gauziest of fans in a gaudy display of skin.

"Felix!" Maya bound from the bar and bounced up to me, clutching my arm. "I didn't know you were coming."

"Rehearsing a new act," I asked. Friendly as ever, Maya'd become rather attached to me, being the only person to interact with her in, well, she won't tell me how long. Loneliness does things to a soul.

"I didn't know they had a stripper night." Molly eyed Maya up and down, judgment dripping from her pursed lips. Being generally invisible the last few hours had loosened her tongue and emboldened her facial expressions.

"You can see me!!!" Maya jumped up and down, a flowing white dress cascading to cover her curves. Her bounding hair suddenly Marilyn blonde, the whole ensem in homage to the classic *Seven Year Itch.* Reading was a problem, but movies were not. Maya'd had a lot of time to herself.

"You can see me?" Molly jumped in excitement, all judgment gone from her face.

"She can see me?" They turned to me simultaneously.

"Yes," I said to Maya, still gripping my arm. "Yes," I said to Molly, *now* gripping my arm as well. "And no, she doesn't count," I said to both, forestalling their next question.

Maya-lyn pouted her now red lips.

"How'd you do that?" Molly asked Maya of her quick change.

"Oh, that's nothing honey," she said, puckering her lips for a kiss. "Just put your lips together and blow." No whistle, a jarring bullhorn instead.

"Ahhh, what the actual fuck," Molly covered her ears.

"Little warning," I said, rubbing mine.

"Sorry, Felix hun," Maya said. "I've been a bad girl." She tee-heed. Then cracked a whip, suddenly in leathers.

She put the whip handle under Molly's chin, who lifted startled eyes to meet Maya's now looming gaze. Her boots, stilettos, Maya grew taller still.

"I see you're new here," Maya said. "Smell fresh," she inhaled. "Staying long, hun? We could have some fun."

"She's not staying, Maya," I said. "But she'll be around. Wanted to introduce her."

"You've figured a way out then?" Maya's golden eyes lit up, trying to divine the secret of escape from Molly's being. "Tell me, tell me," Maya hissed in low whisper close to Molly's cheek. "Felix won't." She shot me daggers.

"I don't know," Molly clenched. "He won't tell me either," she said. "Sorry." This last was genuine as Molly placed a hand on the frazzled Maya.

She flinched at the touch. Unused to sudden connection, Maya vanished.

I could faintly hear sobs coming from the bathroom.

"Was that..." Molly began, her memory stirring.

"From the night you thought I ghosted you? Yes." Molly had heard strange things that night. "Believe me now?" I'd told her all about it, but it had all seemed a little far-fetched.

"Starting to," she said. "Can I change like that?" She faked a sneeze and her hair went purple. "Ohmigod," she fingered her frizzy purple locks. Strikingly familiar.

"Whoa now." I needed to rein Molly in quickly. "You'll lose yourself and get stuck like Maya."

"Stuck?" Molly's focus lapsed and her hair poofed back to its natural auburn — at least I think it's natural.

"Stuck," I repeated. "Maya can't get out."

"Because you won't tell her like you won't tell me," Molly snapped. Fear and anger taking control. "Why won't you let her out? Do you like having some shapeshifting tart fawn all over you?"

It was nice, I had to admit to myself, but that was beside the point.

"Maya has lost herself. She doesn't know who she is anymore. Can't maintain her self. Notice how she changes quick as thought? Flickers through faces like she's swiping left," I said, laying it all out. "She forgot her face trying to get noticed."

"How long has she been stuck?" Molly shifted between anger, fear, and concern. She had a good heart.

"Too long," I said. "She won't tell me when she got twisted.
I imagine it's been a while." If she remembers. Sometimes
remembering is hard.

Molly slouched to the bar, a bit deflated.

"If *she* can't get noticed with all that," she said, waving her
hand. "How do you expect *me* to get noticed?"

The fear was real. If Molly didn't figure it out soon,
she could start coming unthreaded, spooling out like a
tattered sweater. She was a smart cookie though, she'd come
through.

"All that," I said, "her acts? They get noticed. The crying in
the bathroom, the bagpipes drifting along empty halls, the
screaming flash of red bolting off the escape?" I listed off
Maya's biggest hits. "She's the ghost behind all the stories
you heard about this building. Maya. But no one notices
her, connects to *her*, grounds *her*... because she doesn't even
notice herself anymore."

I let it linger, silence magnifying the impact.

"She's gone about it all backwards," I said at last. "I can't
help her," I said, "but I won't leave you," I tried to reassure
her. "You'll figure it out."

We sat.

We sat at the table she had claimed that first night, months
before. I ordered the drinks. No barflies bothered Molly.

Maya didn't come back. I don't know if she heard my tirade.
Part of me hoped she did and figured it out. I'd like to know
what she actually looked like.

We sat. We drank. Lola, with the ever-helpful name tag,
asked if I had a hollow leg. I laughed. Molly drank some
more.

She slouched over her beer. Empty like the rest. Like she apparently felt. It was hard for me to watch her slip away. I couldn't.

"Tab out," I called to Lola, handing her my card.

"Whisky! Make it a double," Molly shouted in vain. "She can't hear me. No one can hear me. I'm going to be stuck being a ghost tart," she rambled on as Lola brought back the slip for me to sign. "Promise me you'll keep me company when I'm a ghost tart, Felix." Molly was well and truly toasted.

"Now you be safe tonight," Lola said. "You got a ride home," she asked. "You've had an awful lot tonight and hollow leg or not..." she'd begun clearing the empties, stacking glasses on her tray.

Her cleaning nearly done, I bumped the table as she reached for her pen, causing it to fall.

"Promise me, Felix," Molly said as, out of habit, she snatched the pen and handed it to Lola.

"Thank you, hun," Lola said to Molly. "I see you've made a friend, Felix," she laughed, turning to me. "Little young, isn't she?"

I smiled. Molly, though, Molly absolutely batshit lost it. Laughed so hard she couldn't breathe.

"She okay?" Concern stretched across Lola's face.

"Yeah," I said. "She's going to be just fine."

The Stretching Hour

THE HOUR THAT STRETCHES. The hour that winds.

The hour that blesses. The hour that binds.

I've done this before. I've done this again.

I know exactly what's coming as I open my eyes.

Every damn time.

She's not there. She's never there.

Eleven after eleven, ante meridian, I wake to a cold bed. Lonely. I look to my left where she should be and see *Spring's First Blush* hanging on the wall. Today it wore its fall colours — adding the u in her honour — tree turning the boulder into a ginger.

That's how it goes. Every day since my memories started seeping in. Knowing I was once happy pained me. Knowing I'd chosen to forget hurt worse. Or so I thought. I couldn't remember.

The shower hissed, drenching me in fire. I bent and stretched. Bits went crackle and pop, especially my neck. One good twist and it cracked like a tray of ice cubes. It felt glorious.

I let the water wash over me, thinking, my mind lingering in what little it remembered.

I'd paid a lot to forget, it felt like, more than I bargained for, but it didn't hold. Asshole was good enough, though, that I couldn't remember how it'd happened and who owed me a damn refund. I only had one clue from the Count, a recipe I couldn't make. Yet.

"Fat lot of good it did me," I mumbled, wiping the fog from the mirror. I swiped a comb through my hair and looked at the handprints beside mine. Smaller. Delicate. I don't know who's, but they show up here and there.

I have my suspicions, founded more on blind hope than any evidence. I keep hoping for a message drawn in the mirror. Some sort of sign. I'm not that lucky.

Bling.

Be right down, I text Molly after pulling on a shirt and buckling my jeans. Three missed messages of varying levels of annoyance.

I popped out the door at one, two, three, four on the clock to find Molly squatting by the T-bird's tire, reaching under the fender. I was late, sure, but not steal-my-car-and-leave-without-me-late.

"You think I'd hide a key where everyone would look?" I watched as she smushed her face up against the paint job, tongue sticking out as she reached as far up under the wheel well as her arm would go.

"No." Molly kept on reaching. "Gotcha." She smiled and pulled out a black box covered in mud. A box I had not put there.

I squatted down next to her, looking at the mucky box.

"Wassat?"

"Tracker." Molly slid the cover off and popped out old batteries.

"You're low-jacking my ride?" In front of me no less.

"Of course." She snapped some fresh into place.

"May I ask why?"

"No."

"Good thing I don't listen," I said. "Why are you tracking me?"

"*Because* you don't listen," she said, making direct, disapproving eye contact as she replaced the tracker in the T-bird's wheel well. Ah. She was still mad about Vegas.

"I'm touched." I flipped my key ring around my finger and hopped in.

"In the head," Molly ribbed, taking her seat. "Onward," she giggled, pointing forward.

I backed out of my spot.

"Ass," she huffed. We were mostly back to where we'd been. I was thankful.

"I'm not hopping curbs in the bird, thank you very much."

"Mmm," Molly frowned at the map on her phone. I assumed she was waiting for a blip marking our location to show up.

"Not even going to try to be circumspect about it?" Molly had decided she was a fixture in my life a while back. Rather much like a cat, really. A stray who'd adopted me.

"Nope," she smiled at me, flipping her screen to show the tracker was active.

I sighed. She had me pinned. It was a declaration of terms. I could easily do something about the tracker, but she'd know I'd done something about the tracker, and since she'd made sure I knew about it, that'd mean a blatant disregard of her opinion on the matter. I sighed again, not quite sure how to feel.

It started to rain. Swish.

Trapped, something inside me whispered. I wasn't sure where it'd come from, but I didn't like it very much. It felt like a grease spot on my thoughts.

"Speaking of cats..." I started. Traffic was thick today. Swish.

"Who said anything about cats? Left here."

"I did," I said, "in my head," I grinned, inching forward toward the turn. "Didn't you hear me?"

Click. Click. Swish.

"Why would I...nevermind." Exasperated and slightly puzzled. "What about cats?"

Click. Click. Swish.

"Wasn't important..." I trailed off, watching the car in front of me, also turning. I chuckled.

"What?"

Click. Click. Swish. We crept forward. Click. Click. Swish.

"Blinker's synced," I said. "And the wipers."

Molly looked, but the moment was gone. Lost to time past. It may have come again, but the turn came before it could.

There's a tension to it. Everything moving in unison. An edge palpable in that moment. You can't look away until you break it, or it's broken. Synchronicities are nigh on hypnotic, and can be dangerous, as they figured out on Broughton Bridge.

"Break step." I shook my head to clear the mesmer. Swish-swish. The rain picked up.

"Sorry what?" Molly'd been absorbed in her phone, unaware of the lock step.

"Where are we going?"

"I don't know, you're driving," she went back to whatever was so interesting on the app thingy making her screen flash.

"You just said to go left!"

"Testing the tracker," she pinched and zoomed. "Good signal." Flick. Swipe.

The speed with which she flit about the various and, daring redundancy here, sundry apps on the device was boggling. In the span of time it took to inch down the block, I watched her swipe out five texts of varying length — ranging from a simple *lol* to a lengthy treatise on natural gas line repair —, order new shoes for later pickup, and briefly skim restaurant reviews on Yelp. I thought I saw the name Mallorey's flash by, but I couldn't swear to it.

That seemed like ages ago. Another life. But no, same one drawing on. They run together after a while. Don't ask me how I know that —I couldn't say — just one of those things I know.

Like these synchronicities that keep popping up. They connect us, on some level, to the world around us. The sufficient accumulation of coincidence is never that. The question is not what causes them, rather you need to wonder what message is trying to get your attention.

"Moonlighting as a gas repairman," I asked, quirking my eyebrow and giving her the side eye. "What building are you trying to get into?"

"It's like plumbing, but on fire!" she gleed, pyretics dancing in her eyes. "And I'm sure I don't know what you're talking about," she turned her nose up dramatically, then back down to her phone.

"You're unusually intent on that today." She was addicted, but I'd never seen her so firmly glued to it.

"Just making sure," she said, taking a page from my book on crypticism.

"I think the tracker is working." I saw the dot match our position pretty faithfully.

"And I can still read."

Ah. She was worried about accidentally twisting — slipping askance of reality.

"You'll be fine," I reassured her. "You know what to feel for now. Any purple sparks?"

"No." Molly's eyes lingered on the screen before looking up to mine. "But how can I be sure?"

Fair question.

"You can't," I said. Best to be blunt about it. "Nothing is sure. That's why I made sure you could get out on your own. You have to live your life, Molls."

"Don't call me Molls," she snipped, glaring daggers.

"Making sure you were with me," I forestalled the coming wrath. She put her phone away.

"Let's go there." I pointed the T-bird to a parallel spot, stopping us in front of an antique shop. Wasn't the best part of town — the bars on the windows kind of gave that away — but that's always where the fun stuff happens.

Dryden Antiques, the sign proclaimed in lettering made to look old. The ornate gothic block style font with curvy embellishments — straight from what people think a saloon looks like — also graced the glass of the front door. The modern chime that announced our presence broke the illusion. It didn't even have the decency to sound like a canned chime. Just a two-note Bee-Bong.

"Oh, hi," the clerk said from his compromising position. "This is awkward."

"A smidge," I said, observing the rapier point before my eyes, which then traveled down the blade to the man holding the bell guard in one hand and what appeared to be a Tang Dynasty pottery bowl in the other. The bowl was filled with cereal and milk, which was sloshing over the sides. But wait, it gets better. He wore what appeared to be a wizard's robe — or maybe a monk's, I'm not sure — without any pants.

In this fraction of a second, I'd stopped short as Molly ran into me from behind, stepped to the side, and yelped upon seeing the nearly naked man.

In the background of the darkened shop, I heard the soundtrack of an adventure film playing and the clicking whir of an old school projector which suddenly made a popping noise followed by the thwapping of a broken film.

The smell of burnt celluloid reached my nose.

"Well, there goes a fortune," the fellow grumbled a tad blithely as he sheathed one sword and covered the other. "Come on in," he turned.

I almost turned as well, but to walk out. Molly had other ideas.

"Do you normally greet customers at sword point?" She ignored his nakedness for the moment. "Heck of a sales tactic."

"Wasn't expecting customers," he said as he shuffled away. I hadn't seen a name tag yet, though the clerk — I assumed he ran the place — didn't exactly have a good spot to pin one. But he did have bunny slippers, I now noticed.

"Antique business that slow, huh?"

"Oh, I haven't had anyone walk through those doors in..." he paused, cocking his head to the side to consult the wall of ticking clocks, "nine years, thirty-two days, six hours, and forty-two minutes. Give or take."

Ticks and tocks in rippling waves, just out of true sync. Time marched along the wall of clocks, tightening.

He twitched a bit. "Well, there was that cat that wandered in a bit ago. Sometimes a bird," he brightened.

"Damn man, how do you keep the lights on then?" Molly spoke as I watched the tocks tick closer together.

"Made a great sale yesterday," he said. "Suit of armor if you can believe it!" He laughed with the look of fondness one has for old memory. "And the day before that this lady comes in and buys every taxidermy I had. Even the bad ones."

Molly and I shared a look. This guy didn't look nearly old enough to have worked at any job for a decade, much less have dementia. Barely in his late twenties by my guess.

"Look ou..." my warning came too late but was unnecessary as the vase from the high shelf shattered to the floor where the clerk should have stood. Saved by his swift sidestep, he averted disaster.

"Sometimes I just let it hit," he muttered, slurping milk from his Tang cereal bowl.

"I'm sorry?"

"Oh, don't be," he waved off the remark, "it's not your fault." He puttered off, hopefully to put on some pants. And maybe a name tag.

"Felix, look at this!" Molly had wandered over to the massive wall of clocks. Of every description and variety. There were grandfather clocks next to their granddaughters. Anniversary clocks with their spinning weights. Wall clocks, kitchen clocks, old alarm clocks with shiny bells. One cabinet had a quicksilver pendulum, the shiny liquid metal lapping side to side in the clear glass tube. Also shiny was a small clock surrounded by a gleaming metal sailboat rocking side to side.

Molly, however, went straight for the cuckoos. Who'd have thunk, right?

"Look at these carvings!" She was in heaven, looking at the detailed miniature buildings and figures which would soon dance. The ripples grew tighter as the hour quickly approached.

My eye was drawn to a clock which seemed older than the rest. The brass of the box was dull and scratched, scuffed terribly on the right side, but beautifully engraved. On the left was Fortune, or so the engraving said, a winged woman holding the spinning wheel of fate. To the right, the Fool, who doffed his cap in a jester's bow. Balls hanging in the air around him. In his hand, held open, the winding key. Surmounted with a bell, the hands crept onward around the astronomical dial.

My heart beat in time with the ticking of the clock. I felt it in my hands. Pressure rising as the ticking tocks grew closer apart, the hour drawing nigh.

On a hunch, I held the clock up, inspecting the bottom of the enclosure. A lion, rampant to the right, engraved in the brass.

Cuckoo-cuckoo-cuckoo the clock near Molly chimed, breaking the oppressive tension. I had not noticed I'd been holding my breath until I let it out with a gasp.

"Sorry," she shied, "I couldn't wait." She'd turned the hands five minutes ahead, triggering the mechanism.

"Play it again," I smiled. "I missed it."

"You guys might want to leave," our host said, returning from his putter. His eyes nervously flicked over all the clock faces. "I don't know what will happen now," he said, giving me a run for my cryptic money.

I quirked my eyebrow, still holding the brass clock.

"I've done this before," he continued. "I'll do this again, but no one's been here when the clock strikes. This is new." He looked confused.

Molly looked to me, alarmed.

I looked to the clocks on the wall, ticking away. And laughed. Idiot.

"Oooh, look at this one," I said, going over to a Rhythm musical clock. I moved the hands to trigger the music. The numbers on the dial spun about in a waltz of time. "And this," I triggered another cuckoo. And another. Setting time free.

"Feeelix," Molly looked scared. She felt it, too, now that she thought about it. Knew what to look for. Good. I needed to show her.

"It'll be okay," I smiled reassuringly.

The clocks struck, but now not all at once. I looked to the clerk whose eyes went wide and mouth agape as they silenced their song, ticking once more.

"I'm free!" He jumped up and down, doing a little jig. "I'm free! It's after two!"

"You're new at this, aren't you?"

"What do you mean?" He stopped dancing.

"This," I waved at the clock wall. "Time is a wild thing," I said. "It doesn't like to be caged. Bad things will happen."

Blank stares met my explanation.

"You stick this many clocks on a wall and let them sync up," I said. "Or worse, *you* synchronize them on purpose," I left the accusation hanging. "It's like an iron cage, each resonant tick reinforcing the trap. You gotta let time breathe, man."

"I thought grandma was just superstitious," he said, working it through.

"Nope, do as grandma says," I advised. "How much?" Changing the subject, I held up the small brass clock that had caught my eye.

"Take it, man," the grandson said. "Take all of them. I don't want to see a clock ever again."

Glimmering Lights

"CHUG, CHUG, CHUG," DAMIAN and his crew chanted over the band at Beckett's. They'd gone full Nintendo this Halloween. Damian in a red hat and fake stache. His boys matched in green, yellow, purple hats and coveralls with equally ridiculous staches glued to their faces. He'd even picked up a Peach since I'd seen him last. Guess I wasn't the only one who liked blondes. Pretty, her fruffy pink dress took up half the bar as she made sweet talk with her Mario.

The other half was taken up by a DK chugging beer from a barrel. Great costume for the big guy who wore it. Another recent addition to Damian's crew, I was given to understand. A good nine feet tall in the costume, fur from the neck down, conceivably to hide stilts, with the classic red tie around his neck. Beside him on the bar was a gorilla mask.

"What's on tap tonight," I asked as I bellied up to the bar to get a Scotch. I was feeling classy in my pinstripe suit, slicked back hair, and a stache of my own — not exactly fake. Plus it fit the image with my fake cigar.

"Felix!" The giant ape man belched appreciatively. "That, sweetie, was a tasty brown ale," he said, putting the barrel down for a refill. In his hand, it looked like a normal stein, but next to my newly delivered Scotch, you could tell it was a keg.

I toasted Damian-Mario at the end of the bar, he flashed down another hundo telling the bartender my Scotch was on him. So was the barrel of beer. A few more chugs like that and I worried Beckett's taps would run dry.

"What'd I tell you?" I cocked my head toward the big guy and smiled.

"You were right," Damian laughed. "Where's your Morticia?"

I looked around the crowded bar, then back at the door. No sign of Molly yet. No text saying she'd be late either. She was probably getting her costume perfect.

"Not sure," I shrugged. "Cara mia'll be here soon." I had faith. "You guys seem to have hit it off," I changed the subject. "Glad you could come out, Sassy."

"Famously," Sassy-pants said. "Damian's the only one besides you who can keep up," he laughed. "Almost." No lie. Sassy could drink us both under the table volumetrically, but that's why he used a bigger mug going one for one. He drained his barrel and slammed it down, DK style. "I love Halloween!"

Just about the only time of year he can really get out of the woods. He'd even gotten a shave for the occasion. Sassy was stylin' with some chestnut brown Farrah hair lookin all Fabio with his strong chin and angular nose. That's what his barber Nicole said anyway. She does right by Sassy.

"I love your costume," Molly chimed in from behind, slipping in between me and Sassy. "Sumptuously soft," she stroked the fur.

"Ooh honey, be gentle!" Sassy-pants shivered at the touch, eyelashes fluttering as he looked down at the non-Morticia-Molly. "Eee, I love your hair," he stroked her bright green hair in turn, feeling it between his fingers. "Who does it?"

"I did!" She coifed her cascading waves of green. "New friend helped me out, though," she smiled coyly. "Monster blood," she called to the bartender, leaning forward.

It wasn't just green. It was many shades of green. I'm sure they all have names, but green is green, here with verdant variety. Also, it was a lot thicker and longer than it had been yesterday. Suspicious.

"What happened to Morticia?" I eyed Molly up and down, looking all slutty dryad — because most Halloween costumes tend to be slutty — with the hair and leafy green-gold corset pushing everything up top and vines lacing up her arms. Total mismatch to my Gomez.

"Wasn't feeling it. Too hot for all black," she smiled. "Besides, this is much more me," she flipped her new hair. Actual hair, not a wig.

"Quite fetching," I appreciated, knowing what she'd done. "Boobs got bigger, too," I observed, fishing for confirmation.

"Felix!" Sassy choked on the next chug.

"Helped me get noticed," she winked, squeezing her chest as the bartender brought her drink. Oh lord. "Nice stache," she added, eying me over her glowing green concoction, completely on theme. A preemptive counter to my forthcoming lecture.

She'd cheated like I had, changing in the twist. Coming out different than she'd gone in. I wasn't happy, but I held my tongue lest I slip into hypocrisy. When had she learned to do that? Now I knew why she hadn't texted.

"Girlfriend," Sassy started, "don't ever think you need big titties to turn some heads you pretty young thing." He gave me a stern look. "No matter what *some* may say." One that said *Mhmm, I'm talking about yo sorry ass.*

"Why thank you," Molly bubbled. "Felix, introduce me to your handsome tall friend here," she pressed against Sassy's arm, barking up the wrong tree.

"You've met, actually." I sipped my Scotch while she fawned.

"Pish tosh," she affected. "I think I'd remember."

"You drank too much." Suddenly I felt a tad taciturn. Spiteful? *Never.*

Thought bubble burst followed shortly by my eardrums. Molly gleefully squeed as she jumped up and down, threatening to bounce free. I guess she figured it out.

"Calm thy magnificent titties, Molly," I drolled, knocking back my whisky. "Sassy-pants doesn't like to draw attention."

"For real?" Molly looked back and forth between us, eyes sparkling with wonder. "Real real? Not a costume?" She reached out to touch the fur again.

"How rude, I have a magnificent costume on," he said. "Best one here! See?" Sassy waved his red tie in her face and grinned.

While Molly glommed on to Bigfoot, awake and still sober this time, I slipped out for a breath of fresh air. Hopefully she got a selfie sans thumb this time around.

My face itched.

I scratched at it, wondering what was wrong when my hand encountered the Addams stache. I checked myself in a passing store window. Good resemblance to the Astin version, I thought as I stroked the new hairs. Pointless. My mood soured.

I rounded the corner and twisted back to my self as I turned. It didn't really matter which I wore, they were all costumes. I stretched and cracked my back, feeling my shoulders ripple back into place.

Molly seemed to have picked up on that — that the self was more than physical appearance. I was a mixture of proud and terrified at the revelation. I *just* taught her the baby steps and

she just skipped right to esoteric grad school. They grow up
so fast.

I wiped a fake tear as I wandered down the street. Molly
was right, it *was* warm for late October, I had to admit.
False Fall had lingered a tad long and Summer's Second
Coming burned with a vengeance at being delayed. Real talk:
Morticia's clinging black dress would be unbearable. But
damn she was letting it all hang out. "Plus what she'd added
on," I muttered, remembering her new boobs.

Roarious cheer drifted down on the welcomed breeze. The
Bigfoot bar crawl wasn't the only festivity going on for the
spooky season — not that normies would know that was
even happening. Blazing bonfires were lit to drive off the
non-existent chill, a beacon on the hill for all to see. People
flocked to the makeshift market, in costume and out, and
bobbed for apples and took turns in the pumpkin patch lined
with lanterns. Tent stalls had sprung up at the crossing of
paths where children lay in wait.

"Boo!" One such jumped out wearing a Batman mask, laying
my way while the rest gathered round singing a chorus of
"Trick or treat, smell my feet, give me something good to
eat" while holding open bags.

"What is this, a stick up?" I laughed and held up my hands.
"I ain't got nothin, honest," I played along.

"Awww," seven year old Bats began.

"But you do," I knelt beside him, reaching for his ear. "Got
something stuck right," I twisted my wrist, "here," and
dropped a Snickers in the sack. Full size.

"Whoa." The kid gasped at the newfound riches.

"Careful now," I whispered close, "they may get ideas you're
a Bat piñata."

Bats went wide eyed and bolted. The rest of the treaters gave
chase.

"A way with words, you have," a familiar voice from behind. "Come, come, see what sooths need said." 'Madame Zestra' beckoned me over her crystal ball. "Cross my app with silver and ye shall know," she waved to a code.

I'd gotten practiced at that since my last encounter with Deirdre and her spirit guide. Entering the tent, I booped her some digital money from the cloud or wherever it comes from these days. A soothsayer and prognosticator on All Hallow's Eve. Not foreboding at all. I thought vaguely about being surprised, but wasn't.

Cha-ching.

"Seeker, ye be, I see," she waved her hands over the crystal ball which clouded now, purple. Great effect. I can appreciate talented craftspeople even when I feel they're grifting me. Game recognizes game. "Darkness looms large on your horizon."

Not a happy fortune then.

"I see," she paused. "I see," her eyes squeezed shut, her back arched. "I see the threefold death awaits," she deflated.

"Oh," ah well. "Welp, how do I go?" Hate to spoil the surprise, but I'd like to have a clever snark at the ready.

"You do not, you wait." Her piercing emerald eyes locked intently on mine. "Death is not for you," she said. "Never you. You who were born on the last day to exist."

What the hell did that mean? Dramatic much.

I waited for her to say more, belabor the point, offer a cure — for a price — but she simply stared. Her painted lips unmoving, jaw tense as if her tongue were unwillingly restrained. Frozen.

"Yoo-hoo," I waved in front of the reader's eyes. "Earth calling Madame Zestra, do you accept the charges?" I reached for her hand — stupid mistake, remembered too late — and flew back out of the tent with a thunder crack.

I saw other skies. Bluer. Truer. Wiser. Skies that watched over me many seasons and lifetimes ago. I saw shadows form and swirl in my wake, polluting and corrupting those whose lives I touched. Those I loved.

And who loved me.

The images emblazoned upon my prefrontal cortex give me pause to this day. Flashes of past, present, and possible future. Jumbled, yet portrayed with salient clarity.

Myself, fingers dancing upon the wind. My wife, brush in hand, face splattered in paint. Molly, her hair white, washing glasses. Minutes striking seconds striking hours.

I digress.

My senses returned to find me seated in Deirdre's tent having a lovely cup of tea placed before my face, as has now become our tradition. Zestra had apparently fled, her crystal covered, and Deirdre had been talking as she'd made the tea and drawn the drapes down around the tent entrance. At least, I presumed she'd been talking since she was in the middle of a sentence I've entirely forgotten.

"Welcome back." Her willowy hazel eyes met mine over the cup curled in her hands. I saw one set for me and took a sip. My throat burned terribly, I was just noticing, and the gentle herbal soothed it. Had I been breathing? I couldn't remember.

Deirdre patiently waited as my cognitive functions resumed, reconnecting to my body. Damn signal disruptions. Her eyes flickered around me as if watching a dozen different TV screens and in them I saw a glimmer of light. Reflections of the other skies I'd seen. Her jaw tensed.

Or maybe I was projecting again. I examined the draperies as I stalled for thought. Lavender silks hung from the tent rails. Maroon festooned the walls. Sterile white from the outside as all festival tents are, the inside she'd made homey. Plush. Carpets laid down against the damp grass, layering over each other. How long did it take her to set up? She even had a tea set for goodness sake.

Her eyes never left me as mine wandered about. Deirdre's mouth upturned in the ever-present smile, still exuding ever-welling positivity. I still found that unnerving. How?

The reader unfolded from where she'd sat — legs having been tucked up to her chest — and lowered her cup, now emptied, to the saucer. Serene and peaceful, her previous tension resolved, she'd gathered her thoughts while mine still fractured and strayed. She tilted her head and reached for a deck, hand lingering above each placed on a shelf, before choosing one which apparently felt right.

Still not a word she said as she shuffled the tarot.

One card leapt. Eager to be seen. Six sharp swords adorned its front, swinging in six crisscrossed arcs, with six flower blossoms falling away.

"A journey, far from home. Distancing. Accept the lessons." Deirdre's typically chipper voice — I'd been watching her videos. Like and subscribe! — took a hollow, metronomic tone.

The third card flew on the heels of the second, landing on the silken table cover with a slide. The second familiar from before — a queen with a star-marked coin in the palm of her hand, upright this time — the third not so much. A lion, jaws spread wide in the grasp of a slender woman. Deirdre's lips quirked a smile.

"Radiant power. Courage, compassion, and confidence follow the Queen. Nurturing abundance and sensibility flow from her power." Animals on both, I observed. The lion marked Strength. A rabbit at her feet, the lush garden through which the queen walked showed signs of more creatures hidden within.

"She's got this," Deirdre said, a bit less monotonic. "Stop hovering and accept who she is. But you got to go," she said, looking up into my eyes. "You'll know when. Listen." She held up the bottom of the deck and pulled two cards for me to see, not looking herself at what they said.

One was an Ace, a single coin wrapped in vines. The other a wheel marked Fortune, set against a star-mapped sky and strung with threads grasped by skeletal hands.

A final card fell to the table, overfull cups set under the crescent moon. Four of them. This she twisted to pour the cups out.

"Get out of your head and see what's in front of you," Deirdre smiled. "Get clarity and choose to be, like, happy." She brightened a bit, her serious streak done. "At least your taste is improving," she grinned, "but she's not for you."

Little did I know.

Lanterns in the Fog

"DO YOU KNOW THE tale of Stingy Jack?" I non-sequitured. I can do that. Make words be words. And thus non-sequitured now exists, and I did it.

"Why are they always named Jack?" Molly had asked a passing pigeon where I could be found. Damn flying rats, always snitching. "Is this one nimble and quick? Carry a lantern?" She skipped ahead and danced around, wild green hair flowing unbound. She'd acquired a cloak — deep red, and long. It rode over her green and gold, swishing as she danced, the fur lining caressing her curves — exaggerated for the night.

"Same dumbass," I said. "All of them. Canonically it goes Jack and Jill, Beanstalk, then Stingy — which made the rest possible." We walked along the stalls at the fest.

"Okay," Molly allowed. She examined some crafts, thanked the maker with a smile, and bounced on. Stopping for a sweet.

"Stingy Jack was a gambler," I began, knowing where to this time. "Terribly bad at it. Never learned his lesson from the beans, but then he also wasn't quite right after that crack to his head." I shook mine sadly. "That was sort of remedied when he traded it for a pumpkin, though."

"Upgrades!" Molly shoved her newly acquired candy apple in the air as she twirled in delight. Or maybe she'd tried to keep up with Sassy-pants. Regardless, ebullience flowed.

Her spirit was intoxicating in its own right.

"Where was I?" I spied a booth to visit and angled toward it. "Right. Gambling. Terrible at that, but, as a trickster, he was great. Learned a lot from the bean guy there. So when he lost his soul on a bad run of cards..."

"He lost his soul?" Molly interrupted around munches.

"To the Devil, yes," I went on.

"'Ou can wews eor souw?" Her lips tried to smack free of the sticky.

"Easily," I waved. "Huge black market for 'em. Not the point of the story. The point is the tricking." Molly's eyebrows rose but she remained quiet.

"Stingy Jack scrubbed the back of his neck, embarrassed he'd lost his soul to the Devil like an idiot," I said, laying the scene. "So he asked him, he said: 'Now Devil, you won it fair and square, ya can do with it what ya will, but can I at least say goodbye to my wife and kids?'

"And the Devil — used to being on the deceiving, not on the receiving side — the Devil, he said: 'Why sure, Jack, we'll have plenty of time together.' Not counting on Jack to welch on the bargain, what with eternal damnation on the line." I'd slipped into my best storyteller oration, drawing unbeknownst on years and years of practice.

"But he already lost his soul? Why *wouldn't* he try to get out of it?"

"Well now the Devil has seven levels down in hell," I said. "First few aren't too bad, that's where Jack would have gone. So the Devil didn't think...."

"Always a mistake," Molly chimed in. "What'd Jack tell his wife and kids? That must have been a whopper."

"He didn't tell them anything because he made them up," I said. "Sympathy from the Devil. Stalling tactic. Either way, the next day the Devil came for his due and Jack, well he said: "Now Devil, I'm ready to go an' all, but can we have one last drink up here?"

"'Oh, why not?' the Devil did say. 'Tempting the Devil himself! I'll make a fine Devil of you yet, Jack.'" I led Molly past the rows of Jack o' Lanterns set out on hay bales. Each carved by one of those masked hellions running around while at school.

I picked one up and held it in front of my face. "'Cheers to that, Devil,' Jack toasted and drank with the Devil.'" I shoved the lantern closer. "The tab came round and Jack patted his pockets, turning them out."

"Maybe he didn't believe in physical money?"

I pointed straight at Molly. "No skipping ahead," I chided. "'Devil,' he said. 'Seeing as you're taking my soul and all today, I gave it all to my wife and kids,' — he left out the part about them not existing — and he looked around. 'Maybe 'an we could skip out? Poof-gone?'" I made the wavy magic fingers at Molly like Jack did the Devil.

"'No, boy. I always pay my debts,' said the right honorable Devil. And he transformed himself into a gold coin right then and there to pay the barkeep."

"How's that honorable?" Molly stopped and thought. "That's totally, like, counterfeiting, right? He's just going to transform himself back after the barkeep is paid, isn't he?"

"Well that was the tricky Devil's plan, but Jack pulled one over on him," I pulled a coin from nowhere — shiny and gold — holding it between my fingers. "Jack took the coin," I motioned, "and put it right in his pocket where he'd stuck a silver cross he lifted off a preacher."

"Holy shit, he did not!" Molly burst out laughing, almost folding double. What a beautiful sound. What a beautiful view. Distracting.

"He did!" And I pulled out my new coin wrapped up with a cross. "'Now Devil, don't be cross. I just did what any'ould do. But I'll set you free if you don't bother me,' Stingy Jack said, albeit loath to part with a gold piece." I disappeared the coin again, the cross dangling free.

"He just let Jack go?"

"'For a year and a day, no more,' the Devil did say. But that wasn't the end. Three times Jack tricked the Devil, until at last he wanted Jack no more."

"Clever," Molly said, as we passed a graveyard on my way to our destination. "I bet it came back to bite him, didn't it?"

"Always does," I laughed, a bit ruefully. "Always does."

"Samhain Blessings," the white robed woman said — pronouncing it correctly: sow-en — as she carved a turnip. Her booth banner read 'Practical Witch Supply.'

"To you and yours," I nodded. Molly struck a notion to curtsy, spreading her hands as she dipped her still green head. Molly had not changed as I had, and I hoped she never would.

"What's with the turnip?" Molly picked up one of the fat faces the woman carved. I perused her table while the blesser explained.

"They are the traditional lantern for Jack," she said. "Last much longer than a pumpkin, they do. Stouter and don't fall in on themself like a drunkard gourd," she almost spat the disdain. "Shrink and shrivel is all," she waved down the line of shrunken heads.

"Ohmigosh, we were *just* talking about him!" Molly spun a turnip in her hand, examining the scowling face. "The stingy one," she clarified.

"A good tale, that," the professional witch nodded. "Heed the warnings, and be not like that fool Jack."

"Why not?" Molly laughed. "Yes, he was stupid to bet his soul, but he got it back?" I hadn't finished the story.

"Aye, of a sort," she considered. "But that's not where it ended."

Molly turned on me and I shrugged. "You walked too fast."

"Well how's it end?" Molly held a lit turnip in one hand, the other on her hip. She looked back and forth between myself and the advertised witch. "What's with the lanterns?"

I deferred to the lady in white.

"Fool boy tricked the Devil alright," she started, "making him promise not to take his soul, and the Devil always keeps his word."

I poked at the witch's crafts on offer besides the turnip lanterns as she finished my tale – the part that rankled me. Knotted wards and spelled candles. Lovely charms. All sparked effective.

"So, Jack did keep his soul?" Molly tried to follow the scattered threads.

"Only by default, you see," she said. "Jack was a terrible man. Horrible. The gambling and stinginess was just putting it nicely."

"Okay?" I saw Molly trying to fit the pieces together.

"So when ol' Jack died," the witch went on, "he wasn't taken to Heaven on a flight of angels' wings."

"So he went to Hell after all?" Molly guessed wrong.

The unnamed witch shook her head. Names have power, I remembered, and she was wise not to wear a handy tag.

"No, love," she said. "The Devil keeps his deals, I said, and wouldn't take Jack's soul."

"Then which way'd he go?" Molly was growing concerned by this point, though I think it'd clicked already.

The witch waved her hand, Molly's attention drawn.

And I'm an ass.

"Baaahahahahahaha," I jumped out at Molly with a flaming turnip held high.

"Felix, you ass," she screamed and hit me.

I said I was.

"He's not half wrong," said the witch. "Ol' Jack haunts the dark places — the forgotten paths and deep woods — with only a hellflame coal to light his way."

"Stashed in a pumpkin?"

"Turnip," the woman reminded. "Much stouter," she nodded, "as I said."

"As you said," Molly echoed.

While Molly was mildly enchanted with the fable, I found my eye drawn to several carved wooden instruments. Pipes and whistles. A goat-skin drum. In particular, a flute felt familiar.

"Elder wood," the witch followed my eye. "Do you play?"

"Not that I recall," I hedged. I did a lot of things I didn't know about.

"Give it a try," she encouraged.

The flute in my hand gave off a charge — imbued with something. I felt no malice, but it's never wise to just fiddle with a strange flute. First off, that's not how they work — you faddle a fiddle and flaut a flute. Second, I had no way of knowing just what the charm would do.

"By new gods and old, it will do you no harm," she assured, seeing my hesitance.

I ran my fingers over the delicate carvings twining round the flute, fingering the smooth holes. What the hell, worse had happened to me. I blew.

It's easy to say a lot of worse things have happened to me, especially in retrospect, more especially because nothing happened at all. Absolutely no sound came from the Elderwood. And yet...

"Gyaah," Molly clamped hands over ears. "Stop that hideous shrilling." She grabbed the flute from my hand. The smiling witch in turn took it from hers.

"You've a touch of the blood, don't you," she asked of Molly. The witch took the Elderwood flute and slipped it into a velvet purple bag.

Does she, now? I thought curiously of all the things Molly brought about. Hazel — because I didn't have a name, and sometimes I'm not clever — came to me with the velvet bag, placing it in my hand.

"A gift," she said, "one of future need," she forestalled my objection. I don't like gifts. But I shut my trap at that addendum.

"Aww, don't give him that!" Molly protested. "He's going to screech it at me just to be obnoxious," she pouted.

"He obviously needs practice," Hazel smiled, turning her eyes to me. "One day he may play for you beautifully." I wondered how I could play a thing I could not hear. One only Molly could.

Hazel bid us blessings as I tucked my new gift away against the future need. Molly flounced ahead, skipping to a loo. No doubt sloshing after meeting Sassy.

Here's a lesson for you kids: Don't knock on stranger doors. Trick-or-treat be damned.

I'm getting ahead of myself, telling this all out of order.

Molly and I found ourselves in the woods. Behind the loo, we spotted a path untrod. This untrodden path carried us past low gravestones — mossy and worn — forgotten, almost, to a door standing at the edge of the wood.

Simple and plain, well crafted, stained a dark walnut brown. Just the door upright in its case, standing ajar, no building surrounding it. The front door to something, once — nothing now — opened into the misty woods.

Merry light danced in her eyes as Molly waltzed through the open door before I could stop her. I sighed and followed, knocking thrice to be polite.

Manners matter wherever you go.

The fog had grown thicker as we passed shadowed trees reaching out, further graying the world of silver moonlight. Obscuring everything around us. I felt no twists or fuzz. No indication we'd got turned around in somewhere other, but we were lost.

I kept walking, not saying as such, while Molly began nomming a confectious treat. My eyes scanned the shadows for some beacon, some bearing.

"Where's your costume," she asked as we trod deeper in the fog. Her lush green hair contrasted against the pink cotton candy she now ate. She'd gotten the last of it from a vendor — his name tag called him Gary — as he closed up for the night. Molly'd tucked the bag under her cloak. For later, she'd said.

I supposed now was later enough. In answer to her question, I snagged some pink fluff and pointed to my own handy name tag.

"That's it?" Molly leaned over to read the engraved name.

"Does it really matter? They're all costumes." I walked on.

"That's not even your name!" She jogged ahead of me and spun, her long cloak twirling as she did.

"That's the point," I said. "Tonight, I'm not Felix."

Further ahead, a light grew in the darkness. A way out perhaps? The glowing embers of the festival bonfire?

"Remind me to reconsider my stance on fae traps if we get out of this." Molly ducked a low web, careful not to disturb the spider.

She knew? I looked at Molly, my expression neutral, inviting further elaboration.

"The door?" As if that explained everything.

"What about it?" How much had she learned without me?

She darted ahead and spun to face me, walking backwards down the path.

"I wanted to see what would happen," she said. "And nothing happened, well, except we're lost. Aren't we?" Her big eyes met mine, seeking answers. "I didn't see the purple sparks," she added accusingly.

"Because we're not twisted," I said. "Just unfamiliar. A mite bewildered."

"I wasn't sure the door was hinky until you knocked." Molly had shut her bag of sweets for a more-later-later and examined the foggy wood. The light ahead grew stronger as we drew near. "Why did you?"

"Knock? Polite thing to do." The light grew brighter. A lantern to guide us in the night?

I wondered what it was — further away than I thought — and what awaited us, when we came upon a tree — leaves red as could be, basking in the glimmering light of another world. Sunshine filled the night, seeping through from another land, banishing the darkness from within the confines of a wide circle of mushrooms.

"What in the world," Molly wandered to the edge in awe.

"Not in the world," I warned, my hand on her arm. She stopped.

"No," she stretched her neck higher for a better look, "I suppose not. Where then?"

"Somewhere else," I shrugged. I don't know all the planes that exist, just that they aren't *here*. "Boundaries play loose on these liminal nights," I said. "My best guess..." I began, but would have been wrong as a little fairy appeared at the edge of the mushroom ring. Where'd she come from?

"I am here to drink the colors from the leaves, please." The ginger fairy didn't blink as she looked directly at Molly. Not of a height, barely larger than a child, the slight fae held out a hand. Her delicate features were inviting, hair the colors of autumn — all reds and golds with a few purple strands set against orange — plump yellow lips smiled around sharp wicked teeth, glittering eyes black as a night full of stars locked with Molly's.

"What do you mean?" Molly, ever curious, stepped forward. As she did, she slipped a hand into her flowing cloak.

"I am here to drink the colors from the leaves, please," the ginger fairy repeated. Wings of a monarch fluttered then folded behind her. Fidgety.

"I have no leaves. But, I have this treat," Molly offered the pink candy floss. Her off hand gripped in her pocket. "I'll share."

This offer was not well accepted as the little fairy cringed back with a hiss.

"What trick, what trick?" Her eyes darted around, seeking a source of attack.

"No tricks," I said as I lowered Molly's offending hand. "No tricks, see?" I held mine up, empty. To Molly, I muttered: "Put it away. What is given burns the hand."

She hid the intended gift, looking to me for clarification.

"We are sorry to have interrupted your business, small one," I said placatingly. Trying to ease the fae off edge. "She meant no harm."

"Right, sorry. I just thought you might like some of my candy," Molly smiled, trying to charm. "What are you doing, if I may ask?" Damn her curiosity.

"I am here to drink the colors from the leaves!" The ginger fairy perked up, wings fluttering her off her feet toward Molly.

"How," Molly asked the now giddy fae as she landed right at the edge of sunlight.

"You want to see?" I didn't like the sound of that. Her black empty eyes locked on Molly. Hunger glistening among their stars.

"Sure," Molly giggled, before I could say *No.*

Too late, I was, as the sunlight breathed her in. At the tree, I saw them in a blink. Molly stepping forward with the ginger fairy, wings of a monarch folded behind her.

Molly was laughing, her words muffled as they came to me. I slammed into the sunlight wall, trying to break through to Molly.

Blood on the knife. A thought came to mind. *Quickly.*

What knife? I wondered, momentarily setting aside the new voice in my head — so long as it was helping. I had to get through.

I felt a weight settle in my hand as a knife did appear — heavy and cold. Iron, of course. I bloodied my palm upon the knife, looking up to see the ginger fairy turn, yellow lips peeled back over sharp teeth as she latched onto Molly's face. A kiss, not sweet, not gentle.

Molly resisted — good girl — hand pulling something from her cloak pocket. A salt shaker?

"Well that won't work." I squeezed the blood welling up in my hand and smacked it against the sunlight wall. The barrier rippled and crackled, hissing at the touch of blood. I hit it again.

Molly flung the salt at the fairy, seasoning her face to no effect — she wasn't a Devil to blind or bind.

"Punch her with it!" I slapped the wall once more with bloodied palm. "Right in the face!" She'd still feel pain if not from the salt.

Molly wasn't listening. Or rather, likely couldn't as she began to grow limp. Her struggle diminished. The green faded from her hair. Damnit.

I stabbed the crackling barrier with the bloodied iron knife, piercing it ever so slightly. It was enough as the trapped light streamed out and into the forest night, burning the fog away like a roiling flame.

"Molly!" I sprang in, brandishing the knife at the startled fairy. Her feeding interrupted, she fled behind the crimson tree, dropping my friend.

I slid through the leaf litter to catch Molly's limp form.

"Felix?" Molly's voice was weak, her hair stark white. "What happened?"

"Shh," I said, glaring at the ginger fairy peeking from the tree. Oh, how I wished she wore a name tag. I'd do far more than report her to her supervisor. Names have power and fools give them away for free. Instead, I pointed the dripping blade, placing myself between Molly and the fae. "Leave us be."

"I just want to drink the colors," the ginger fairy teared up. "Why are you being so mean?"

"She's not a tree!" I pointed vigorously at Molly.

The stricken fairy's face screwed up in confusion. "Not right now," she protested. "But tree she'll be."

Devil of a Night

WHY WAS EVERYONE TRYING to one up my crypticism?

Seriously. Stop it. That's my shtick.

I admit, I've always known more about what's going on than I've committed to the page — and that's how I like it! — but just a bit more. Just enough to be confused.

And so here I am.

My eyes gritty and glazed. My head pounding as I turn page after page in Lenore's back rooms. The secret rooms. The rooms Marty doesn't even know about, yet somehow I do. The answers elude me.

Before, answers always came when I needed them, too conveniently one might say, and I trusted that. I didn't particularly want to *know* more — felt that way lie madness — but then Molly got hurt.

Molly twisted her way in with a tray of tea. Lapsang Souchong by the smoky smell. There appeared to be proper biscuits as well — I mean cookies. Maybe scones? Things are muddled. What country is it?

"You should be resting," I want to say but my throat burns. How long had it been since I spoke? Molly beat me to the punch.

"Break for tea?" She motioned with the pot, steam wafting from the spout.

My throat, too dry to protest, croaked. I nodded instead.

Her white hair had stuck. Everything else about Molly had gone back to normal — said she was tired of the flouncing and back pain from the boobs — after our Samhain misadventures. Except... she felt less.

And it was my fault.

"It's not your fault," she objected to my unspoken thought. I glowered. Molly smiled. "You're staring at the hair again," she added. "Shall I pump up the ladies to give you something better to stare at?" Molly bounced a bit, her chest inflating to near cartoonish size as she leaned over, handing me my tea.

"Stop that," I waved her off. Taking my tea to sulk in the dusty corner of the twisted room filled with books others should never see. "You don't need to lose yourself any further."

I stared at the spines before me as I sipped my tea.

"I know who I am, Felix," Molly assured me. I had my doubts.

I felt her eyes boring into the back of my stubborn skull as she sipped from her own cup. Studiously, I avoided their gaze, finding the gold embossed titles eminently fascinating.

Natural Philosophy next to *The Lesser Key of Solomon* and *The Gospel of Mary Magdalene* and many others in languages I could not read, but that tickled my fancy.

I picked one at random to flip through.

"What's that one?" Molly had been perusing my odd selections laid out on the table for study.

"I have no idea," I said, quite honestly. "Just feels right."

I opened it to a page at random — about what I'm not sure — when a note fell out, distracting me from the contents of the book.

The single leaf of paper — or was it parchment? — fluttered quickly to the floor, neglecting the typical somersaults one expects of paper in the air currents, slid along the boards in its enthusiastic dance with gravity, stuck under Molly's toe. She crouched to retrieve the missive.

"Careful, Felix," Molly said, holding the presumed page gently, "that one's shedding."

"No." I closed the book and stepped closer to take the sheet from her hand. "It was tucked inside. Loose, not part of the binding." I missed.

"Extraordinary," she breathed, holding it closer to her face, out of my grasp. I'd seen script on it and, more peculiarly, a familiar green lion, rampant, illuminated upon it as had been on my invitation to Vegas. "May I see it, please?"

"When I'm done," Molly snipped. She smiled playfully and batted her eyelashes as she did when she wanted her way. Before, it had been cute. Now I found it slightly irksome. I breathed, pinching the bridge of my nose. No, it was the anxiety bleeding through — hers and mine.

"It looks like letters," she went on, returning her attention to the note.

"It's an old script," I said. I'd caught a glimpse of the calligraphed message, though not what it said.

"Not that," Molly squinted. "That's easy: 'When the pupil is ready, the master will appear,'" she read. "See here?" Molly pointed to squiggles that looked like water flowing, tracing the shapes outside of the text, within the drawing.

R D N M B T H W C L S 1 0 & 4 5

We copied the letters and numbers we could find on a scrap of paper, roughly in the order found.

"They're all consonants," I observed.

"What is this, Welsh?" Molly giggled.

No, not Welsh. Something else came to my mind. It was like Hebrew, but using the English alphabet, formed into...sigils. The word filled itself in from the fog. I began plugging vowels in at random, trying to decipher the gibberish.

We stared intently at the page, Molly and I leaning close, trying to make heads or tails of the message. Letters had begun swimming in my eyes when an orange tabby landed square on the page we'd been working on, demanding attention.

"Elliot!" Molly scooped him up and scratched the cat between the ears. "Where'd you come from?"

I swept the ciphered page into my pocket. I'd take another crack at it later. For now though...

"I think he's saying it's time to close up," I petted the cat. "Aren't you?"

"But..." Elliot jumped down as Molly motioned vaguely around us, mrowing in protest.

"But what? Cats can go anywhere." I left it at that, feeling better about my crypticism, and stepped out of the twist.

She didn't ask if I'd found anything. She didn't ask if I'd had any new theories. She didn't tell me if she'd had any new symptoms. Outwardly, only the hair was apparent, but inwardly...she was losing time.

A few days after the ginger fairy drank her colors away, I'd found Molly basking in the afternoon sunshine, the warmth caressing her face as the chill wind ruffled her hair, she sat very still as squirrels played on her lap. It was a very Molly thing to see, but it was different. She'd seemed dormant.

Afterward she'd had no memory of the day passing or why she found nuts stashed in her hoodie pocket.

I didn't know what was happening to my friend, and she didn't ask — not that I could do a damn thing to fix this. Instead she put on the chipper bright face I'd come to know so well the last year or so. Had she always been hiding this? She seemed fine last winter.

"You're doing it again," she chided from the passenger seat. "Stay here," she said. "Be in the moment, not in your head." It hurt, but she was right.

It felt like she was dying. Felt like she knew it too.

"Sorry," I mumbled. We'll see about that. "Where do we want to drink?"

"Anywhere I didn't hit with Sassy," Molly laughed.

"That really limits our choices," I feigned a grimace. "Sassy gets around."

"Does he ever," Molly rubbed her head. "And I thought Elder could drink!"

"I keep telling you guys, but you don't listen." I flicked on the wipers as rain started to streak through the headlights. "How is Elder anyway? Haven't seen him in a minute.'

"Oh he's off in Alaska visiting family," Molly said.

"Long way to hoof it." She laughed, kindly, at my bad joke.

"Got a postcard while you were in Vegas." Molly sighed a touch dramatically, casting a sideways glance my direction.

"I sent pictures." A touch defensive, sure. I was doing it for her protection.

"One!" Her head snapped toward me, white hair flailing. Stark contrast to her red leather coat. "One picture of a stupid pigeon-masked guy getting pooped on."

"Not my fault they arrested me." I said it under my breath, grip tightening on the wheel. "Stupid pigeon."

"And none of it would have happened if I'd been there," she harrumphed. "Do you know what could have happened to you all alone?"

"I was fine," I said. When had she become so fretful over me? "I wasn't exactly alone."

"You think Bunny — was that what you called the stripper? — would have bailed you out?"

Not everything stays in Vegas. I'd told her a little bit about what went down. Not all of it, but I had to tell her something.

"I was fine. No Bunny needed. I had the cash." Could have walked right out, too, if I'd wanted — but that tends to raise more questions than I have answers.

"Lucky you had that much," Molly said. "Could still have that money if you'd let that St Germain guy talk them out of the charges."

"I don't like owing favors," I said. I hadn't gone into those particulars.

"What's his deal anyway?" The way Molly bounced topic to topic put me in mind of a songbird flitting about just then. Beautiful, but fragile. "He seemed quite the character from what you said." Molly's laugh trilled magically. "Super bombastic!"

"No, that was Paracelsus," I said before the thought fully formed.

"What?" Molly's eyes crinkled questioningly as she tilted her head, just looking at me.

My mouth worked uselessly. I had no idea what it meant.

That'd been happening more often than I'd have liked —
words that I had no idea were in my brain slipping out to
play. Ever since I'd started poking my nose into subjects that
were probably better off left buried in my past.

Who was Paracelsus?

The more pressing question though was who in the hell was
this flagging us down in the pitch dark night? The poor soul
must be soaked, standing by what looked to be a moped.

"Did he break down?" Molly's attention flitted to the fellow
shielding his eyes from the headlights. Older, hair matching
Molly's, but scraggly and unruly as it stuck out from a
woolen cap. Bent, now — he might have been tall in his
youth — clutching closed his coat, trying to keep the rain
out. He was not succeeding. "Pull over, Felix, he needs help."

Where she got her brashness, I haven't a clue, but it was nice
to see it hadn't diminished. Still, danger stranger he may be.
Before I could exercise any sort of precaution, or even say
we should, Molly wound down her window. Rain spattered
in.

"Hi," she beamed. "Can we call you an Uber or something,
sir?" Always with the apps, handy as can be.

"Oh, no, no," he shook his head, shedding drops, "nothing so
fancy," the man dissembled, shuffling closer to the T-bird.
"Outta gas, maybe a ride to..." he paused, looking at the
two-seater, "ah, ah, no. No room." He turned away, one hand
shaking, ever so slightly.

Molly made to get out of the car. This time I was quick
enough, stopping her from unbuckling as I called out. "Sir?
Sir!"

Against my better judgment, I got out, cold rain pouring
down my neck.

"You just need some gas?" The gentleman turned back as I called over the T-bird's ragtop.

"Yes, old son, did I stutter?" He laughed. "You got some?"

"Should." I didn't, actually, but I could cheat, walking back around to the trunk.

"Why you ridin' around with gas in the back?" I twisted the key in the lock as he came up. Features cast red in the tail lights, the old man's bushy eyebrow raised. "You wanna blow up?" Long shadows crept up his face as he reached to grab the can.

"I'll get it." I snatched the empty red can before he could. The old metal clanged hollow against the trunk lip.

"You sure you got some gas in there?" He shuffled toward his moped as I closed the lid, locking it back. "Can looks old as I am. Mighta done evaporated by now."

"I just keep a little in it," I shook some slosh into the can. "Kaboom bad, sure, but gauge's been busted probably since the can was bought," I grinned in the scant light, "and sometimes I guess wrong."

"Sir!" Molly popped out of her door at a run. "Please, take this." She splashed to the old man and held out an umbrella. The one I'd gotten her after she'd taken chill dancing in the rain at the Huxley.

"Okay," he said, taking the gift. "Thank you..." he paused for a second.

"Molly," she held out her hand to shake.

"Hank," he tried for her hand, "Hank Daniels," and missed, trying again. "Happy New Year," he flustered, finally gripping Molly's fingers awkwardly.

Bless you and your kind soul Molly. It was just the distraction I'd needed to cheat. Now get in the damn car before you catch your death.

"All filled up," I said, drawing Hank's attention as he stood silhouetted in the T-bird's headlight.

"She's alright," Hank cocked his head back toward Molly, who, thankfully, was getting back in the bird. Whether she'd heard my unspoken thought or just had good sense, I didn't particularly care. But let's chalk it up to good sense. "I'll give you a dollar ninety-eight for her."

Didn't quite have an answer for that.

"The car," he added at my confusion. "You look familiar." Hank carried on while I tried to catch up. He got on the scooter.

"No, and I think I'd remember you," I laughed. Hank was a character.

"You do, just not now." Hank turned in his seat and checked a case strapped to the back. Violin, unless I was mistaken. "Left the fuel pump on," he said by way of errant explanation. I thought.

Hank puttered onto the road and I waved.

"I'll see you there." Hank waved back then popped open the umbrella against the rain. A mighty odd thing to say considering I didn't even know where we were going.

"He said he'd give me a buck ninety-eight for you," I told Molly as I got back in. Straggly white hair clung to her face as she tilted her head and squinted at me.

"And what'd you tell him?" She turned, pulling a towel out of nowhere as she stared me down. Damn, she was a quick study.

I winked and cranked the T-bird.

"Said I needed at least tree-fiddy," I memed, putting the car in gear.

"Got damn Loch Ness monster," she replied, solemnly completing the ritual before giggling. "*Is* Nessy real?" She asked no one in particular as she dried her hair.

The rain gave way to fog, seeping among the trees as the bird's lights swept through the boles. Feathery fronds from the ferns reached out into the road, marking the edge.

I didn't rat on Nessy. Instead I asked. "So where are we, aside among the fog and ferns?"

"I dunno, you're driving," Molly poked a corner of towel into her ear.

"Yeah, but you're tracking me. What's the app say?" I kept on going up the windy road, going over an old iron bridge in the night. It felt strangely familiar to me and I didn't like that at all.

"We are..." Molly began, pausing while the map loaded. "Huh, that's strange," she said as I saw the wheel of death spinning on her phone. "No signal, but at least I can read it." Always finding the bright spot.

"Exactly nowhere, then." I took a left. Then another. And a right. Roads appearing, none of them crossing. I thought I knew where we were going and it made me anxious. I kept my face calm, neutral, while something else nagged at me, prickling the back of my neck as I was drawn along.

We never passed Hank.

Logically, we should have — and rather quickly. He was puttering along on a moped with an open umbrella. Not exactly aerodynamic — but there was no sign of the strange old man. He couldn't know me...even if he did before, that was the old me. Must've just been confused. He didn't seem all ther...

"FELIX LOOK OUT!" Molly braced against the dash, instinctively trying to mash the brake as a shadow leapt across the headlights.

I swerved.

There was no thud. No cracking of glass. No indication at all that we'd hit something.

Molly looked back wildly to see what had jumped to find nothing.

Only shadow.

"Do you ever wonder if mice look up at bats flying in the sky," I distracted, loosening my grip on the wheel, settling my pounding heart, "and think they're angels?"

"What?" Her wide eyes locked on mine. She'd seen something in the shadow.

"Der Fledermaus," I said, bucking my teeth and fluttering my hands by my face. "Rats with wings."

"No," she looked at me like I was stupid for even thinking it. "They think bats are loud ass annoying fuckers who can fuck right off with their damn screeching. Damn ultrasonic bastards."

Of course Molly would know. Probably quoting a mouse-friend verbatim.

"So they're more like bass thumpers?" I put the bird in gear and drove.

"Yes," Molly nodded. "Universally despised. Should I be worried I still don't have signal? I mean, we're not twisted, but..."

The turn threw me. She was scared. Her brave-faced gumption had run out.

"No," I said gently. "I know where we're going now." *I think*, I didn't say. I didn't like it, but the familiarities were falling into place.

Molly accepted the answer. Trusting me. It hurt.

We were headed to the Last Chance.

The Last Chance

NOW, AS THE NAME might imply, this is where you go when you've lost all hope. It's not anywhere you want to be — unless you're a special kind of stupid — and you don't end up here by choice. Only by chance, your last one.

Diviest looking dive bar, it sits at the crossroads of Ben Hurt and Height of Despair where lonely and doomed souls pass by. Come untethered from the world and their earthly form, wandering and waiting. Blazing neon cut through the fog, lighting the way as the T-bird's beams swept over an array of conveyances.

I felt sick at the thought of leaving Molly here, felt like I was abandoning her to the fate I'd been trying to avoid all along, but she was running out of time and I was desperate. She needed a safe haven, even one among the lost.

Shit cars, beat up old trucks, bikes of every variety — pocket rockets, Harleys, bobbers, customs with ape hangers. I thought I even saw a Schwinn.

"As good a place to drink as any," I said, parking next to what looked like a horse. "Now play nice," I told it. Molly did her thing and...

"He's not talking." Wide eyes took over her face, shocked.

"Not surprised," I said. "Not a horse." I walked past it, spying a familiar ride down the line.

"What do you mean it's not a..." She didn't finish her thought as the black steed snorted, tendrils of flame escaping flaring nostrils. Blue blazes danced in its black eyes. "Oh," she quickened her step. "Oh, oh."

Molly knew and loved animals, but she'd learned her lesson about this variety with the not-a-foxes.

She's grown so much, I thought, *and so fast.* I looked at her admiringly. *Faster than I can keep up.* That thought pained me.

"What?" Molly caught the look. "Something wrong with my face?" She stuck her tongue out and crossed her eyes.

"Nope, still as perfect as ever." I chuckled and headed for the burly brick wall guarding the door. Much rather face that than Molly's reaction.

The bouncer ignored me and I ignored the bouncer. Unstoppable force. Immovable object. Yadda yadda. Dismissive? Me? Nah.

"You stink of Lethe," Princess challenged me. No handy name tag here, but he made it too easy, wearing an honest-to-goodness crown. His nostrils flared and his thick brow furrowed.

"And you stink of yesterday's tapioca," I said, "and fish," and smiled. Memories rattled loose at the mention of Lethe, but I pressed on. "Great, now that that's out of the way. Get out of my way."

A meaty hand pressed against my chest, stopping my entry. But barely, much to his surprise. He seemed the sort of goon used to having his violent way. Sorry to disappoint chum. The expression staring down at me wasn't so much disappointment as murder. I smiled back, looking up at his crooked crown of shining gold, so out of place on him it made me laugh.

"What poor head'd you pluck that kids meal crown from, Princess?" I felt ripples run up my spine, anticipating a swing. Part of me wanted it. The violence. Somewhere deep and forgotten. You don't live as long as I have without a few scrapes to show for it. Why did my mind go there?

"At least he bathes, Your Highness," a weathered voice laughed behind me. Familiar. He *had* said he'd see us here. "How are you, Garth?" Warm mirth filled the voice in the dark.

"Mr. Hank!" The bouncer snatched the crooked crown off his head, stopping short of bowing. "Well, sir, thank you," The effort to not straight up genuflect seemed to pain the bruiser. "This lemming with you?"

"They helped an old man out when he was broke down," Hank said, clutching a case to his chest. "Thank you for the loaner." He held the damp, nearly folded umbrella to Molly with a tremoring hand.

Ever the consummate grifter, Molly read the situation and took the proffered umbrella, stepping in closer to take the old man's arm and kiss him on the cheek. I thought I heard a whispered word — *thanks.*

"Ahaha! She kissed me!" Hank smiled in doddery delight. "You see that Garth? She kissed me."

"You're a charming devil, sir," the bouncer stood straighter in Hank's presence, holding the door for him. "It's good to see you, sir," Princess Garth said as the pair passed, Molly helping Hank over the threshold.

"Rudolf," Garth grunted as I followed, "second one." I quirked an eyebrow. "You asked. I answered." He let the door hit me in the ass before I could ask more.

"What's a lemming?" The question drifted back as Molly chatted with Hank. We walked down a hall toward an open doorway. Din and roar flowed from the light spilling out.

"Rodent suicide cultists," I said. "Just a myth, though. Faked."

"Limousine," I thought Hank said. Harder to hear with the approaching noise. "Greek river. Makes you forget."

"Limousines make you forget?" Molly shot a glance at me. I'd have glanced my way too, were I able to bend like that. And were I not distracted by dreams recalled — of a ginger at the ferry...bridge...whatever it was.

"That's right," Hank laughed. "Lemmings take a drink, wash away trouble and care, catch a ride back. Here we go," he said, passing through the doorway before either of us could ask what the hell he was talking about. To the side of the frame, I noticed a lantern. Empty, bearing no flame. Made of sooted brass, etched with a figure I couldn't make out.

On the other side, a woman stood in the dim light at a high top to the right, sipping a dirty martini

At first glance, that was that, but a look closer revealed she had ashen grey skin shot through with shimmering splotches. Her sharp, pointed teeth clanked off the glass as she drank — seemingly new to her mouth. Stem of the glass nervously held in talons, afraid she'd snap it like a neck. In place of olives or even onions, two skewered eyeballs garnished the drink. One winked as we passed.

She spotted my attention and turned, hiding her face behind a mass of frazzled hair any 80s band would be proud to front, revealing the sharp spines protruding from her back that prevented her from sitting.

"Nice place," I said somewhere between sarcasm and general non committance. I sidestepped a waitress with three arms — one to carry the drinks, one to serve them, and the third to seemingly stab any hand coming near her ass, as evidenced by the bloodied dagger. Someone'd pulled back a nub.

"Used to be great," Hank said, slightly agitated. "Gone to shit!" He sidestepped a drunk flying through the air, landing on the table next to us.

"What happened?" I surveyed the chaos and confusion of the barroom floor. People and not-people milled in violent reverie. I think I even spotted the — or what looked like a — redcape from the maze and was careful to avoid eye contact. I didn't think I had any coins to spare right then.

"Lost a bet," Hank said, walking across to the bar. An opening in the madness formed around us — rather, more likely Hank, if the bouncer's reaction was any indication.

It bothered me — the reverence.

One burly guy with three eyes punched a balding cyclops in a plaid shirt, sending him sprawling. Only...as Hank drew near, Triclops there grabbed the plaid and spun ol' Oneye out of the old man's slow path. The guy juggling flaming daggers? He almost backed into Hank, not paying attention, before some kind of winged lizard bit him in the ass and hissed.

The whole charade smacked of Maya. At least, the shit she pulled around the flatiron. It was all a show. A mockery of a demon bar.

"Mr. Hank," the barkeep nodded as she polished a glass. Even that seemed put on — most bartenders don't just stand idly polishing glasses. Plus, she had horns. Horns that seemed to nag at her, and goat ears to match.

"Evette," Hank giggled preemptively at the joke he was about to make. "Nice rack." Mischief twinkled in the old man's eyes as he sat, carefully placing his case on the bar.

Evette's ears twitched and blood red lips sneered. Her handy name tag, though, read Azalith.

"They're horns, not antlers," she answered primly. "I don't like them." Her lavender pale face soured.

"I think they're quite fetching," Molly brightened, sliding on to the stool beside Hank. She wasn't wrong. The horns were sleek, sweeping back through slicked, short red hair, following the curve of her skull nearly to the nape. Purples shot through the red.

"See Evette? Molly likes them and she has great taste." Hank said. "She kissed me!" He pointed to his cheek as if to prove his point.

"Please, sir, it's Azalith now," Evette spat the name on her tag. "You'll get me in trouble."

Hank's eyes darkened for a second before his easy smile returned.

I turned to lean back against the bar, surveying the resumed chaos. Whoever had orchestrated all this had taken great care in crafting every detail.

"So how do you know Mr. Hank?" The glass she'd been polishing filled with whisky she'd spirited from somewhere unseen.

"We..." I began to say *don't*.

"They saved a poor old coot by the roadside!" Hank interrupted, shooting back the whisky.

A whisky appeared at my elbow, Evette/Azalith's green eye meeting mine. One for Molly as well, though she was too busy steadying Hank. I raised my glass and drank. A sweet Crown for Hank.

"Any friend of Hank's," she said.

"To Hank," I raised the glass.

"Two dollars!" Hank said. Still on about the bird? "Good silver, too." He flashed the coins between his fingers.

"I'm not selling you my car," I laughed. "Or Molly," I grinned at her.

"Damn right you're not," she shot back. "I'm not anyone's to sell. Hmph!" She flicked her head to the side, whipping her white hair around and shot back her glass, turning the empty upside down.

"Damn." The response I expected from Hank came instead from EvAz, no longer looking at us. She paled.

"Azalith," a sonorous voice said. The entire bar fell to hushed stillness. "Since when do we serve anything *neat*?" Crisp white shirt, casually unbuttoned at the top, he appeared from a door of hidden shadow.

He felt wrong. Menace radiated from the very presence of what approached. It looked like a man, but...empty. Devoid of anything resembling humanity. I felt sick. Molly gripped at my shirt, but I couldn't look her way — my eyes locked on the preternatural threat. Instinct screamed to run, but wisdom said this creature would give chase.

EvAz stiffened as he stepped behind, far too close. His eyes hidden behind the glare of gold rimmed glasses. His shadow loomed large despite his median height. Ominous. Imposing.

"I'm sorry, sir," she squeaked. The 'sir' was laced with fear, not respect as it had been for Hank. I liked this *thing* even less.

"Where's the style? Where's the panache, Azalith?" He slammed his palm down on Molly's empty glass, sending shards skittering. "Where's the grotesque delight?" He raised his palm, bloodied glass embedded in the meat, and licked it. Ruby eyes winked at me from his cufflinks.

"Yes, sir, it is lacking in all these things," she demured, eyes lowered.

"Leave her be, Hector," Hank came to her defense. "Evette did it for me, for old time's sake."

"This isn't your bar anymore, it and everything in here belong to me. Her name is Azalith, now, old timer," Hector snarled, "and I am now called Xe'elathon." He actually sneered, the over dramatic bitch. How many apostrophes was that?

"I'm not calling you that fool name, Hector," Hank phahed, waving the foolishness off. "And she'll always be Evette," he settled back onto his stool, crossing his arms. Contrarian surlyness oozed from his manner as only an old man can muster.

"So long as I own the Last Chance, she is Azalith." The sneer deepened, then gave way to bemused greed. "Should you wish a rematch, though," he waved an upright palm, inviting Hank to make a move.

"Lord Sale-a-thon, sir," a pale creature appeared crouched atop the bar with a bowl of soup. Androgynous and shriveled, hunched with spines along its back, and sharp teeth in rows, the creature bowed its head and held the bowl out with one gnarled hand. "Your kraken bisque." Though it sounded like the minion said 'bishth,' what with the mouth full of fangs. Probably why they'd called the boss a car sales event, too.

A boss who seemed to take it as a personal affront, judging by the veins bulging at his temples, just below his swept back hair. Malevolence surged in the air and his shadow grew darker.

Hector-Sale-a-thon snapped, his coal black shadow lashing out, covering the poor server in darkness. And gone. The engulfed soul simply vanished. The shadow, it seemed, was the true threat, not Hector.

It wasn't right. None of this was right. I couldn't leave Molly at the Last Chance, not like this. It was no safe haven, not anymore. It was a trap. A feeding ground for the wicked and depraved. Revulsion replaced fear.

There was only one thing I could do: something stupid.

"Hey Sale-a-thon," I got wound up, "I'll take your challenge." My gaze leveled with his as I rose.

"And who the hell are you?" The weight of his sudden regard made me flinch, just a bit, as his shadow roared like a bonfire. Hector cocked his head as if listening and smiled. "Him? No matter," he adjusted his gold glasses, "you're black booked. Besides, with that tattered soul, you've nothing of interest to wager."

It irked me, this shadow knowing about me when I barely knew myself. And as far as I knew I was in possession of a perfectly fine soul. Before I could be offended on my own behalf, his eyes traveled to Molly.

"Unless you'd care to part with this tasty looking scrumpet." Hector's shadow stretched out toward her white hair, "what's left of her."

"Excuuuuse me? No," Molly smacked the shadow-hand seeking to cop a feel. "I'm my own person. Not some *strumpet* to be bet or sold." The shadow withered in her glare.

"I like her," Hank came up beside me, back a bit straighter. "Here," he held out his precious case. "I'll stake him."

That shocked Hector. Lust and greed filled his eyes at the offer. Whatever the case contained, it held great value.

"You place your fate in his hands?"

"I trust him," Hank said. "Name a game."

"Darts." The quickness of Hector's response begging suspicion. Intuition said he'd have an edge in that.

"Not with that shadow you've got. Blackjack," I countered.

"Do you take me for a fool?" Hector laughed in my face. Melodic and deep, he threw his head back, leaning into his persona. "No. I think not,", he leveled his eyes to mine for a glower.

Guess he knew I could count better than the rest.

"Dice," Hank put forth.

"Dice," I agreed. It tasted right as I said it. I knew a few tricks.

"Devil's Dice. Agreed. One hour." Hector turned his back and left, his shadow lingering after. I felt it staring at me. The malevolence from it I'd felt before had either abated, or I'd grown used to it, or I was just mad beyond ration's reach.

"What's Devil's Dice?" Molly asked. I didn't know, just hoped I could cheat.

"Liar's Dice. Played with the Devil," Hank said. "Basically. Uh huh. Be nice to have this place back," he changed the subject.

"I haven't won yet," I said. Needed a strategy doing just that.

"You will," Hank puttered to the bar again. "Always do. It's going to be great," he said to Evette.

"It would be nice, Mr. Hank," she risked agreeing, tossing her lot in with ours. "Hasn't been the same without you."

"How'd it used to be?" Molly propped herself up on the bar, bright and chipper in the face of peril as always.

"This place was a sanctuary," Evette said, dropping the Azalith demeanor as she polished another ever-present glass. "A calm place to get a drink and think. Mr. Hank let you just be your confused selves until you settled on one," she said wistfully. "*That one*," she spat, refusing to say the name, "forces us into this," she gestured at her demonic guise, "or *that*," she pointed to the smudge on the bar where the soup bearer had been.

"How did that awful person get this place?"

"Hector cheated. Stole it from me," Hank spat. "Now this guy'll get it back," the old man pointed at me with his drink, still sipping Crown.

"Why Felix?" Molly's curious eyes darted between us.

"Is that what he's going by these days?" Hank turned and looked me up and down. He may appear doddering, but his eyes were astonishingly clear. And deep — the kind that see things oft unseen. "Hm, never have guessed it. Don't look like a Felix, but I guess that's the point, huh old son?"

"That sentence has so much to unpack." Molly blinked, digesting the words Hank laid out.

"You know me?" The dark edge to my tone startled Molly.

"Of course! I know all the jackasses who've beaten me, there's only three." Hank jabbed a finger at my chest. "You're one. Another's right over there," he pointed in the direction Hector had vanished.

"And the third?" What other esteemed company was I being lumped into?

"Doesn't matter." Hank tossed back the rest of his whisky.

Funny. All that drama and fright and impending doom, and no one was talking.

No strategizing. No plotting or planning. Hell — we didn't even go over the rules.

We sat in the numbness while the whole theatrical charade of a demon bar went on. That's how it goes though. Whatever problems you face — life gone turvy then topsy, crashing down around your ears, an entire future crumbling to dust before your eyes — the world turns on, pausing for none.

And in a blink I stared down at a hand full of sixes.

Five six seven.

"Eight sixes," I bet. Opening absurdly high.

"Do you even know how to play this game?" Hector studied me. I shrugged in the silence. We'd moved to a private room for the face off. Only Hank and Molly to witness. And Hector's shadow lurking.

"Call it." I had a plan.

There was nowhere for him to go but up. That's how the game worked. You had to either increase the face or the number or both. Starting out with the highest face, I'd narrowed his moves. There were only ten dice on the table, until one was down to none.

"If you insist," Hector laughed, confident in the win. So was I — the odds said he should.

Oh the fickle whims of fate. All but one came up six.

"Beginner's luck." Hector flicked one die to the side. It landed a six as well.

"Way to go Felix," Molly cheered. "First blood!"

I spread a lie upon my face and laughed. My own luck getting in the way. I couldn't even cheat right, thanks to the creeping darkness surrounding Hector.

"Damn straight." I watched a smile light in Hector's eyes, his shadow rippling with pleasure. He was up to something.

"Watch out for the Devil's Own Luck," Hank had said. Apparently that was the house rule — have exactly three dice left and roll straight sixes. Instant win. "He'll cheat for it. I don't know how. But he beat me with it." Those were the weapons I'd been armed with before facing down the Devil. Well, a devil.

Hector lost so he bid first.

"Six threes." Ambitious, but doable. I watched the shadow for tells.

"Four fours," I played it safe. I needed to figure out how he'd cheat.

"Six fours." Hector leaned back into his shadow — a power move meant for intimidation.

"Eight." I raised.

"Eight what?" I hedged a second, chancing the odds in my head.

"Fives," I said. Two in my hand meant there could only be max six on the table.

Hector had three fives and a one. Outwardly I cursed, inwardly I smiled.

"You win that one," Hector conceded, pushing the one in with the fives.

Shit! Ones were wild. My snake eyes bit. Shit shit shit, I misplayed that. Hector flicked the one away, came up six. He was down to three. Shit.

Zero-point-four-six-three percent.

Those were the odds for a Devil's Own. What I'd been aiming for to get this done quick. Hector beat me to it.

Next round I rolled a foul — two dice stacked up. Too many dice in a small cup. I grumbled inwardly and rolled again. My luck was changing.

No Devil's Own for Hector, but it wasn't for lack of trying — he got two, and won the hand with my three. If only I didn't still have the other dice...

"You finally got me," I smarmed at Hector for show. I knew he wouldn't lose another die.

"What can I say? In the end, I always win." And he won again, taking me down to three.

Overly dramatic bitch. He'd shoot for the instant kill just to be extra. If I didn't come up with the Devil's Own this time round, he'd whittle me away to nothing.

We rolled. My heart sank.

No sixes. I'd have to out bluff this devil.

Luckily, as chance would have it, I'm an excellent liar.

Hector raised his cup, showing a foul of his own. A six on top of two more.

Holy...

"Shit, Felix," Molly dropped her face to the table, looking at the foul dice. "That was close."

Too close. Way too close. My heart was pounding in my ears.

Likely on a lark, Molly puffed out her cheeks and blew the dice over. The top die tumbled, turning over to reveal another six — a second six — as it clattered to the table.

"I knew it!" Hank jumped up in Hector's face. The shadow didn't like that, reaching out to wrap around the old devil. "You cheated! You swapped in two faced dice you two faced liar." Hank struggled against the blackness binding.

"It is called Liar's Dice, originally," Hector slid on a bedeviling smile, pushing up his glasses. "I'm simply keeping to the game's spirit."

He wasn't going to concede just because he'd been caught. Not in his nature. I thought hard. How to flip this...

"I'd offer you a buy-in," Hector tempted, "for this last roll." Scooping the rigged dice into his cup, he shook. "But you've already staked your fiddle for this fool."

SLAM.

"I'll bite," Molly taunted over her turned cup. "You want this strumpet? Beat me."

Hot damn, Molly. I don't think I could have been prouder and yet more terrified at that moment.

"I like her," Hank butted in.

"Me too, Hank," I said. "Me too." Fierce and fearless, and no longer from ignorance, she'd taken her fate into her own hand. Quite literally.

"Ooh, this just gets better and better." Hector flipped down his cup. "No bids, Devil's Own Luck takes it." He met both our eyes for consent.

"Agreed," I said quickly. I knew I'd lost, but it wasn't over.

"Yeah, sure," Molly said, facing down the Devil. But not alone.

I'd lost sight of that myself. Ever since she got hurt palling around with me, I tried to fix her, alone. To find an answer, alone. Never chancing her safety.

But I wasn't alone.

I'd had Molly, and Molly'd just done what she does best — create the impossible.

And now, with the devil's shadow distracted, I did what I do best.

I cheated.

"New sign looks nice." I stood outside Last Chance Molly's, admiring the neon. Already it seemed less loomy and foreboding under the new ownership. Significantly more upclass.

"Ya think?" Molly came up beside me and slipped her arm around me for a hug, her white-haired head leaning against my shoulder. "What the hell do I know about running a bar?"

"Ayunno," I mouthed and shrugged at the same time, garbling the words. "Be nice to people? Help the lost? You'll figure it out. I have faith." She'd do alright.

"Can't you stay?" The plaintive note in her voice almost crumbled me.

"I can't find answers staying here." I'd stayed too long as it was. This was not my place. It was Molly's and she was tied to it now. Already, Molly seemed more herself thanks to the Last Chance.

"Look, you'll be safe here," I went on, filling the silence.

"I don't want to be *safe*," Molly pouted. "I want to be with you. You're fun!" She brightened at the thought of adventure.

"I know, but I need you to be safe." I wanted to say more. So much more. I turned to go.

Molly watched from the door — the lantern now bearing a flickering flame. Her flame — as I walked to my old Thunderbird.

I got down on one knee and reached into the wheel well, feeling around for that mucky black box, pulling it free. I tossed it back to Molly, who caught it in shocked confusion.

"So I can find my way back," I reassured her, knowing she might've thought the worst.

Molly wept.

And the shadow she now cast dried her tears.

Deja Vu

"DEJA VU," I DOUBLETOOK.

"All over again?" Dena laced her arm around my shoulders, pressing against me.

The real Dena, not the painting I'd stared at nearly every morning since the Doyle. Hoping to catch a glimpse of her hair or the sway of her hips. Ever mysterious— though I think it was mostly shyness — she only left hints of herself in her paintings.

We sat on the stone statue's head, watching the sun as it set. The tree blushed pink over our heads as the stars had yet to shine.

"I love this view." Dena relaxed against me. I turned to look at her face bathed in the rose gold rays.

"I tend to prefer this one." I kissed the top of her head. Inside my heart wept because I knew it was not real — only a replay.

"Stooop," she playfully swatted away my kisses, "that tickles."

"Deal with it," my lips said. I was just an observer — my words and deeds set in the life past. Unable to change what was. I pulled her close, hands I could not control tingling at the touch of her warm skin. We were happy.

Why had I wanted to forget this? Was it actually my choice?

I'd wanted answers. Answers only I had. Apparently.

I'd asked Hank — the proverbial devil I knew and who knew other mes — before I departed Molly's to clue me in.

"You already owe favors three, old son." Hank patted the fiddle case that never left his side, reminding me what he'd already done. "You sure you want to add to that?"

That added up. A save at the door. A seat at the bar. A stake at the table. Molly was safe thanks to the old devil, but owing favors didn't sit right.

"I need to know," I said, digging the debt deeper. "Half as I am, I'm no good to her." I looked over at Molly chatting up the customers at her new bar. Her white hair sparkled now and her shadow grew long, grabbing a scotch bottle from the shelf to pour another for a regular. She was getting good at that — using her shadow.

"Seem plenty potent to me." Hank tossed back his Crown. "Seen what you did to Garth."

"The bouncer?" I was wholly confused. What'd Princess have to do with this?

"Ah huh." Hank poked my chest. "He laid hands on you."

"Sure, but..." He'd accosted me. I just didn't take it.

"That ends bad for most," he eyed me up and down, "but not you."

"Cause you stepped in," I said.

"Sure did," Hank said. "I like Garth," he flashed a smile, "and he don't know better."

I took a beat to digest that. Recalculating.

"If you didn't save me at the door, what's the third favor for?"

"Two from now, two from before." Hank held up four fingers, grabbing his pinky to fold down. "One done paid, now three more."

I opened my mouth to ask...

"Neat trick with the gas can." Hank answered the question unsaid, turning to his case — never far away. "Never known how you do that, ya damn cheat."

Hank hoisted the case up on top of the bar, flipping the latches for the first time I'd seen. I couldn't actually see into the case, but golden light spilled out, bathing Hank's face. Gone were the wrinkles, gone were the tremors, gone was the age that bent him — for a second. Long enough for him to slip his hand in and pull out a note. A very familiar note.

"Was asked to give you this should we meet as unwitting friends." Hank's hand shook as it left the light's glow, handing me a rolled parchment, sealed with a green lion.

I glanced down the bar to make sure Molly was still busying about. For a second, I was reminded of our meeting, of how *good* she was with people, how much I'd robbed from her. A second too long.

She caught my eye and smiled.

I smiled back. *Don't come down, don't come down,* I didn't say aloud.

She was coming. I flicked the scroll up my sleeve, my hands remembering the motions.

Motions triggered memories.

The coin clattered to the concrete.

"No, no, no," supposedly-Helena jumped off the trash can she'd been sitting on — one of the big rolling ones. "You're angling your hand too high for the pass."

"I'm just doing what you showed me," I complained.

"If you were doing what I showed you, you'd be doing it right," she countered smartly. "Now pay attention."

She went through the coin trick again — vanishing it and teasing the silver piece back with fluid waves of her hand. No stilted jerks indicative of palms or drops — just dancing the coin about unseen. The trick relied heavily on friction and grace, not mechanical aid — a deft touch was needed. One I so far lacked.

I tried again.

"It's always hiding just where they can't see," she explained the delicate trick. One misstep and...

"Damnit." The coin clattered to the ground again. Why didn't I just...

Just what? Still but an observer, unable to take action. I couldn't move my old hands in the manner needed. They felt achingly clumsy this time around, now that I'd done it before. I remembered the frustration and remembered wanting to do something I used to know.

"You'll get it," unlikely-Helena encouraged, "and pretty soon you'll figure out the easy way."

"There's an *easy* way?"

"Yep." She climbed back up on her alleyway perch with a *hup* and a *hoo*, still mad about my height. "But you only get there once you know the hard way." Her dangling feet swung in time with the clock.

"Nooowww, trryyy too," The words stretched, swimming through molasses, pitch deepening. "Paassssss thhhuuuh cooi..." The rhythmic tick, too, slowed with her words, grinding to a halt. Helena-wasn't-her-name froze in place.

I breathed. I blinked. Burning filled both my throat and my eyes. I hadn't used either, apparently. Not in a while.

The brass clock unwound — stopped a second before nine — the hour nearly done. I felt the fool's key in my hand, itching to wind the spring.

With it, I could live again my past lives, my past selves. Maybe glean more of who I was and gain the knowledge I sought. Hank's delivered missive unlocked the knowledge of the clock, fortuitously come to my possession. There were more, I knew, nine of them with my tenth. Each containing a stolen day.

A day to live again.

That's part of what the scroll had said, more detailed than the others. Who it was from, I still didn't know. Just that whoever kept leaving me these love notes knew what I was, who I had been. The overt script had one meaning, and the artistry concealed another that seemed to tap my subconscious' shoulder.

At least, that's what I theorized.

Every time I looked at one of these green inked illuminations, it triggered bits of my brain. A memory. An impulse. A drive to complete an unknown task.

All *super* unhelpful. Kind of rankled me actually, being controlled like that. But...

I still wound the key, searching for answers in my forgotten past.

"Coin from one hand to the other, like I showed you," still-not-calling-her-Helena resumed at normal speed.

"I'm trying," my mouth said. For the hundredth time I tried the pass, fractionally improving as I did.

"DeWitt." From behind came the strange encouragement. Not from the small round man, rather the parrot atop his head. So used to it squawking "How's ya boy?" I'd almost not recognized the voice.

"I'm doing," I smarmed, waving my hands. "See?" This time the trick worked, to my utter surprise.

The man with the flickering index cards smiled in triumph. His benediction apparently making all the difference.

"You see," he began consulting the cards, "the true secret to doing anything, is just DeWitt."

"DeWitt," the parrot echoed. I'd gotten used to looking down at the significantly shorter fellow, not at the bird upon his bowler hat, since he'd shown me the way, but sometimes the bird wanted attention.

He flipped through several more cards, palming some, sticking another in his mouth as he constructed the scene to be played out.

"My good man," he came closer, "let me tell you about the Distillery on Third. There you'll find the finest apple brandy pennies can buy. It's a short hop," he hopped, upsetting his parrot, "and a skip," he jumped to the side, clicking his heels, "up Northland Street."

"Mm, apples." I liked apples, but hadn't had apple brandy.

"Down the lane and two to the right," he gestured conspiratorially, bringing me in for a whisper, "make a third right for a left and knock." He held my eyes for a moment — one askance to keep an eye out for bumps in the night — then demonstrated on a board pulled from underneath his coat. "Like so." Three raps to the top and one pound with a fist down. "Ask for Sean. There's a good chap."

The board vanished again as he stood straight, tugging his jacket aright, smile plastered across his silly face.

"DeWitt," the parrot said as the man turned to depart.

I watched him for a lingering moment. Not knowing why. Helena-so-she-says stayed strangely quiet the entire encounter.

"Just who are you?" Her eyes re-examined me, slight squint to them. Appraising.

"I'm me," I said with a shrug. "Why?"

"*That!*" She pointed after the parroted man. "That doesn't happen!"

"Sure it does," I said. "It just did. Did you see the pass? How was it?" I changed the subject, not wanting to get into it. She'd acted like she didn't know the guy, even though he'd been the one to send me to her.

"But the parrot..." she wouldn't let go. Fading as time moved on.

The mechanical bird now in view was not a parrot. Rather it was gold with rubies for eyes. Beautifully crafted simulacrum of life.

"What is it?" I examined the mechanism closely, trying to divine its secrets. It sat on the edge of a bowl, twinned across metal water laced with lily pads.

"A timekeeper," the Count of St Germain said, though I knew him by another name then. Younger, hair not gone gray but blonde, no diamond studs in his ear, but there was no mistaking him for anyone else. "One of exquisite craftsmanship and unparalleled precision," he bragged.

I knew he'd made it. His flamboyant personality stamped all over it. His skill in artificing the reason for my visit.

"Remarkable," I flattered, "I've never seen it's like."

"Nor will you," he said, throwing a sheet over the wonderment. "It needs work still. Come, come, what have you for me?"

"For you, a challenge," I said, "for me a favor, if you please." I held a wooden clock to him, careful of its deleterious state.

"You bring me a splintering junk heap?" He examined the piece roughly, unknowing of its origin.

"Easy, easy," I retook the clock. "It leaks time. I need you to remake it, but stouter."

His eyes widened. "This is one of the stolen days?"

I nodded. My heritage. Strange thought I had no reason to think.

"Now *that* was quite the scandal," St Germain said. "Ten whole days stolen right out from under the Pope's nose. Remarkable. Had to make a whole new calendar to cover it up!"

"You have anything to do with it?" I raised an eyebrow, knowing he didn't, but wanting his reaction.

"Me! Ha! I wish. I was staying at my cousin Rudy's when it happened," St Germain alibied himself with a king's vouchsafe. Profligate name-dropper. "Did you, dear boy?"

"I think not," I lied. Even living it again not knowing the truth, I knew that was a lie. "I was just born," I said. That much was true.

The fourth day of the tenth month the year of our Lord fifteen eighty-two. Born on the last day to exist.

The thought echoed strangely in my head — thought then, thought now — a flash of the words from the fortuneteller's lips.

"I can see time right now." St Germain had begun examining the clock with a jeweler's eyepiece — though I suspected there was more to it — one eye squeezed shut while the other peered through the winding key hole.

"So," I interrupted. "Up for the challenge?"

"Give me an hour," he said, carefully removing the viewing glass, considering the rough dial. It wasn't the finest craftsmanship, but they'd made do with what they had.

"That quick?" Slightly surprised until I realized he was bargaining. He'd eyed the clock hungrily, wanting what was inside.

"No, dear boy. The work will take years, like as not." I could see his mind working, already designing the intricate inner workings to conceal the stolen day. The meticulous craftsmanship that would go into each gear, each screw, each spring driving the mechanism. "I mean an hour," he raised the clock, "as my pay."

An hour can stretch to eternity in the right company, or pass like a fickle breeze in desperation. Mine was running out, as the clock wound down once more.

I looked into Dena's eyes and saw the love I'd lost, the friend I'd found, all her incarnations and iterations throughout the years.

I knew myself in her eyes as I'd not known for years. The faces I'd worn, the names discarded.

I felt the trap close around my mind, and for a while, I was happy.

Next Up

CONTINUE FELIX'S ADVENTURES ON Kindle Vella.

Out Now: Fat Chance

Coming Soon: Second Chance

Also By

Vella Series

Felix Chance
The True Tales of Elliot Shaw, Adventurer
Third Time's a Charm

Anthology

"Into the Fire" in *Hidden Villains Arise*

Humor

98 Rabbits: An Assemblage of Words

Sign Up

WANT THE LATEST AND greatest about all my wonderful words and to get an exclusive story?

Just visit: halfacrepond.com/felixchance/

Scan the QR Code to sign up!

My Thanks

THANK YOU FOR DIVING in to the world of Felix Chance. I hope I have entertained you with my words. If I have, please rate and leave a kind word or two so others may find their way to these pages.

About

j.e. pittman is an emerging
author dabbling in many
speculative worlds. He blurs
the borders between genre and
crafts salient lies to tell a
measure of truth. His work has
been described as: capriciously
chimeric, dreamlike, and a
vivid enigma with indelible
images stamped on your brain.
Discover more of his words on
www.halfacrepond.com